apple-polisher

Also by J.T. Holden

Poetry

Alice in Verse: The Lost Rhymes of Wonderland
Twilight Tales: A Collection of Chilling Poems

Fiction

The Boys From Manchester
Three Imaginary Boys
JB: Or The Unexpected Virtue of Being Swaggy

apple-polisher

J.T. Holden

A Kuro Book

ISBN-13: 978-1-937696-22-1 • ISBN-10: 1-937696-22-7

Printed in the U.S.A.
First Edition

To Rachael for loving me,
Dave for listening to me,
Wayne for teaching me,
in spite of all my faults.

How do you like your blue-eyed boy . . .

— e.e. cummings

contents

preface

boy with apple

EVERY TEACHER HAS HAD AT LEAST ONE STUDENT LIKE MICKEY Greenleaf: brighter than average, genetically blessed, confident without coming off too cocky, and resolutely committed to being on everyone's—peers, parents, teachers, *everyone's*—A-list.

A run-of-the-mill apple-polisher.

Gordon Powell, head of the art department at West High, had made this observation five years ago—back when the ink on my teaching certificate still had that freshly blotted crispness and the print on his own had long since faded to a dull fuzzy grey, not unlike the half-whiskers on his cheeks and chin that passed for sideburns and a beard. The only place Gordon's facial hair grew in fully was above his upper lip—and even that hair had developed its own little anomaly. Gordon smoked Vantage cigarettes, or "hollow-points" as he called them, and after years of chain-smoking, his once white mustache had taken on a permanent yellowish-brown hue. Some of the students at West High found Gordon's peculiar mustache to be a source of great amusement and sniggered about it in the hallways between classes; others simply found the man himself to be an infinite source of amusement, derision, and mimicry. Teachers, for the most part, kept their distance—especially those who had been around long enough to know that Gordon, like most old-timers in any given institution of learning, could move huge stones within the administration without breaking a sweat.

I liked Gordon for his frank manner and the way he always seemed to know the answer to any question that was put to him, no matter the subject. I also enjoyed his observations on the students and other teachers at West High—the amusing anecdotes from art class or the monthly senior faculty meetings he would recount over several cups of coffee and a quarter-pack of hollow-points in the teachers' lounge during the free period we shared on Fridays. And in the five years I'd known him, I can only remember disagreeing with him once—and *that* was shortly after his death, so technically, I suppose it doesn't count. Nonetheless, it certainly warrants more than a cursory mention, as I wouldn't have a story to tell if it didn't.

My one and only disagreement with Gordon Powell was this: Mickey Greenleaf was anything *but* a run-of-the-mill apple-polisher.

The boy was undeniably obsequious (though, something in his manner suggested a cool center of control that lay in a sort of half-dignified, half-defiant repose just beneath the surface of his carefully constructed façade). And he certainly knew how to manipulate the supporting players that stood just outside the circle of his spotlight—whether finessing an extension on a long overdue homework assignment out of the most austere of teachers (Gordon himself included), or placating more put-off friends than any person could reasonably expect to divide his time between, or cajoling just about anything his heart desired from friends and casual acquaintances alike (much of this achieved with nothing more obtrusive than a deferentially down-turned head and subtle upward glance from the cover of his strategically tousled bangs . . . and when the situation required that extra nudge, the most effortless and disarming smile you've ever seen).

But Mickey Greenleaf was far from the run-of-the-mill apple-polisher that Gordon had pegged him to be on that warm spring afternoon in the lounge where the two of us sat alone, sipping coffee under the ubiquitous cloud of his smoke.

Of course, I wouldn't come to this conclusion until much later—after I had been asked to sort through Gordon's personal effects in his tiny office adjacent to the art studio at the high school, as well as his only slightly larger one-bedroom apartment on Jackson Street just outside the Canaima County limits.

Only then, after Gordon Powell was no longer available to concede the point, would I realize that Mickey Greenleaf hadn't merely polished his apples: he'd *spit-shined* them.

chapter one

the painting/three letters/the dream

At the time, I would have said that it all began with the matchbook, the one I'd found in the drawer of Gordon's bedside table while searching for a spool of twine. The black matchbook with the Greek symbols written on the inside flap—a coded message that would lead me some eighty miles up into the densely wooded hills of Pierpoint, Pennsylvania, to a Gothic-looking establishment known as The Black Otter, with its sprawling landscape ensconced by the tall trees of the surrounding woods.

At the time, I would have believed this without question.

But in retrospect, I would have to say that it really all began with the painting of the naked boy.

I had received a letter by registered mail from Gordon's older brother two days after Gordon had been discovered dead behind the wheel of his car on the corner of North and Douglas. The gearshift was in PARK, but the engine was still running and the car was pointed in the direction of St. Catherine's Memorial, so it was assumed that Gordon had most likely been headed for the hospital when the final spasm hit. (Some of the teachers at West High are still marveling at the strength it must have taken for Gordon to pull over before losing consciousness, and praising him for putting the safety of others above his own welfare with the hospital just two blocks away. No one ever mentions the pack of cigarettes he was holding in one hand, or the lighter he was holding in the other, when the paramedics arrived. I can only imagine Gordon's disappointment at not getting that last drag in before the clock ran out—one last "screw you" to the heart that had betrayed him after only fifty-nine years.)

The letter from Gordon's brother was brief and to the point.

> *Dear Mr. McGregor:*
> *Please be advised that, as per his wishes, Gordon will be cremated at Kent Funeral Home in Canaima County on May 7th. I would be grateful if you were to inventory his personal effects at the school, as well as those at his private dwelling, and forward any artwork of intrinsic value to the address listed below, along with receipts for any expenses incurred by you in the execution of this task. Any and all other items—including but not restricted to clothing, photographs, books, etc.—I leave you to dispose of at your own discretion.*
>
> *Cordially,*
> *Arthur C. Powell, Ph.D.*
> *84 Ferry Lane*
> *Portsmouth, Rhode Island 02871*
>
> *Post Script: As for Gordon's remains, I trust that you shall dispose of them in whatever manner you see fit.*

. . .

I posted a notice on the student bulletin board for able-bodied helpers to assist me in clearing out Gordon's studio at the school. The sheer size of the job would require at least three people working straight through a Saturday afternoon, and possibly into the early evening, so I added the incentive of extra credit, hoping to entice a few jocks for the expedient removal of heavier items, including seven unwieldy sculptures (four of them carved from huge blocks of stone), a large work table, and Gordon's old dinosaur of a desk.

Five students volunteered for the job—three girls and two guys—which was more than I'd expected, considering that the Saturday in question was forecast to be clear skies in the mid-seventies. The girls—Casey Bellman, Dawn Schroeder, and Alicia Mears—were all from my drama class. The guys—Jonah Phelps and Shane Guerin—were both from my third period English Comp class. Jonah was a skinny kid, eager and diligent, though certainly not a jock. Casey and Dawn were both motivated but, like Jonah, lacked physical prowess. Alicia and Shane were both athletes, so I figured that the three of us could handle the heavy lifting while the other three worked the lighter load.

We started at 10:00 A.M. and had more than half the job done by the time we broke for lunch around 2:00. While Casey, Dawn, and Jonah went to pick up the food, Alicia, Shane, and I moved the last of the sculptures down to the theatre wing and onto the rental truck, which I'd backed up to the loading platform just outside the big garage-style door that opened onto the backstage of the main theatre.

When we closed the truck's rear door, Alicia congratulated Shane for not dropping the sculpture on his foot, and I was surprised when Shane smiled in response to the joke. It was no secret that Shane Guerin, perhaps one of the finest swimmers in the history of West High, was a complete klutz *out* of the water. In the five years I'd known him, I would have been hard-pressed to remember an extended period of time when Shane didn't have a bruise or sprain or broken limb. In truth, my initial surprise and relief at seeing his name on the notice I'd posted on the student board had been tempered with more than a touch of apprehension. All I needed was a trip to the ER with a student under my supervision to make this whole ordeal complete. I could just about see Alicia and me carrying Shane into the ER with his mangled foot hanging askew, while somewhere at the back of my mind Gordon Powell chuckled his deep, throaty chuckle at my complete ineptitude.

Should have just taken a sledgehammer to the lot and swept up the rubble, Jack!

Fortunately, we'd transferred all nine of the sculptures from Gordon's studio to the truck without incident. Of course, it was early, and we still had the desk and the work table to contend with. I pushed that thought out of my head and looked forward to a satisfactory (and safe) conclusion to this day's little outing.

Shane was still smiling when he lifted his T-shirt to wipe the sweat from his brow, and I couldn't help noticing the subtle shift in Alicia's eyes as she caught sight of Shane's bare abdomen. When he dropped the hem of the shirt and met her gaze, Alicia's cheeks flushed, but Shane didn't seem to notice. Though by no means a poor student—in fact, his marks were all above average—Shane had always been a quiet kid, who rarely raised his hand or offered an opinion in class, unless called upon. His social skills outside of the classroom weren't much better. While the rest of his peers were chatting it up at lunchtime in the cafeteria or at the picnic tables on the east quad adjacent to the athletic field, Shane would be off on his own, drawing in his sketchbook, which he was never without, or getting a head start on his homework. On occasion one of the guys from the team would corral him for a sit-down at the swimmers' table, but on most days Shane could be found on the fringes by himself, quietly doing his own thing.

I had initially believed this to be the result of a particularly bad accident, one which had left him in traction and physical therapy for nearly eight months, and forced him to repeat his sophomore year. I'd figured that being out of school for an entire year and then returning to classmates who were all a year younger than he, while the kids his own age had gone onto their junior year, might have caused him to retreat into his shell. But he was a senior now, with none of the pressure of having to see his old classmates on a daily basis, and still he was as introverted as ever. And he was completely oblivious to the attention that one of the prettiest girls in school was showering upon him in her subtle way.

For a moment, I felt like a third wheel, and that possibly my presence was stunting the growth of a possible relationship. I wanted to give them an assignment, a task for just the two of them, so they could have some time alone—send them out to pick up some supplies, whatever. But before I got the chance, a horn beeped in rapid succession as Casey Bellman's powder-blue Beetle pulled into the drive and glided to a stop next to the rental truck. Casey gave me the change from the fifty I'd given her for the food, and we all sat outside on the loading platform to eat our lunch in the sun.

We finished the entire job, leaving Gordon's studio spotless, shortly after 6:00 P.M., and the kids decided to go for pizza and possibly a movie. When Casey and Alicia came and asked if I would like to join them, I smiled. It was flattering that they considered me to be one of them, and though I could easily have passed for a slightly older brother, I was still eight years older than the oldest among them. Hanging out with students for a school-related activity was one thing, but off-campus socializing was another altogether. I thanked them but excused myself due to a prior commitment—which was only half a fib, considering that I still had Gordon's apartment to contend with.

"Did you invite him?" I asked with a nod toward Shane, who was loading the last of the miscellaneous art supply boxes onto the rental truck.

Alicia's cheeks flushed again. She hadn't known that I'd observed her reaction to Shane earlier. I gave her a wink to let her know that her secret was safe, and she smiled gratefully.

Casey said, "He can't go. He has to work."

I was a bit surprised to hear that Shane had taken a job. He was carrying a heavy course load at school and preparing his final portfolio for CalArts (he'd missed the January deadline, but Gordon had sent a letter, along with select samples of Shane's artwork and SAT scores, to an old colleague at CalArts who was impressed enough to give Shane an extension until mid May—a date which was fast approaching). While I admired Shane's fortitude, I hoped he wasn't spreading himself too thin.

"Where is he working?"

"At the sandwich shop just past Highway 80," Casey said.

"Well . . . " I said, thoughtfully, " . . . maybe you should skip the pizza and go for something a little more healthy instead."

It didn't take long for Casey to catch my drift, and a smooth grin broke across her face. "*Yeeeeeah,*" she said, stretching out the word with sly delight.

As Casey ran off to tell Dawn and Jonah the good news, I noticed that Alicia looked even more flushed, but she was still smiling.

There were close to twenty paintings at Gordon's apartment and at least a dozen more that I'd collected from his studio at the school. In all, only six were of the "intrinsic value" that his brother wrote of in the letter. Two by Salvador Dali, one by Edvard Munch, another by Gauguin, and two by a no-name up-and-comer in whose work Gordon had obviously seen enough promise to justify the investment—two grand each, if the final scribbled entries in his battered ledger were correct.

One of these last two was an oil done on canvas made to look like a fresco, fragmented almost to the point of distortion, and very dark. The subject in this painting was a sculpted young man in his late teens, reclining in the nude on what appeared to be an inclined bench press. The boy's arms were stretched above his head, revealing armpits as smooth as the rest of his body. His wrists were strapped to the two metal posts at the head of the bench. A large blindfold obscured the upper half of the boy's face, offering only a shadowy glimpse of his sensual lips, parted as if in a dazed sort of ecstasy.

The subject of the second painting was another young man whose naked body was longer and leaner than the boy on the bench, yet equally sculpted. He sat in profile before a backdrop that hung like a billowing drape caught in a light breeze, his arms wrapped around his bent legs, which were pulled up close to his chest; the lower half of his face buried in the cleft of his steepled knees, the upper half obscured by the silky falling of his long hair.

I had finished packing five of the six paintings in these tall and narrow foam-padded crates I'd found in Gordon's storage unit beneath the apartment—with the full intention of packing the boy-in-bondage "fresco" as well and shipping all six paintings to Arthur C. Powell, Ph.D. of Portsmouth, RI—when I came across the matchbook.

I'd been sorting through the dusty paintings in Gordon's dimly lit apartment since early evening, and it was already a quarter of 10:00 when the spool of twine I'd borrowed from the art department at school ran out. Rather than making a mad dash for the nearest office supply, I took an impromptu tour of the tiny apartment to see what I could find that might suffice for twine—some masking tape, or fishing line, or a coil of thin rope.

A thorough search of the living room yielded nothing more promising than a four-foot strip of braided nylon cut from an old curtain cord, its once fluffy tassel limp and yellowed by the years—a converted cat toy, most likely. Gordon's six cats had been taken in by his landlady, whom he'd worked closely with at the Canaima County chapter of Adopt-a-Pet over the past twelve years. By the look of his scarred furniture and the prevalent scent of sandalwood incense intermingled with the more pungent odors of kitty litter and concentrated urine, I guessed that Gordon had adopted his own fair share of homeless pets over the years. The only scent that rose above all others in this dark and gloomy place was that of Gordon's hollow-points; the ghosts of countless cigarettes still lingered within the folds of the heavy burgundy draperies that blocked out the sun, a smoldering scent which clung to every aspect of the oppressive decor. The bedroom wasn't much cheerier.

Gordon's wardrobe sat against the west wall opposite a matching four-poster bed, the legs of which displayed myriad battle scars from Gordon's army of cats. The bed was just as Gordon had left it the day he died: the duvet and top sheet twisted off to one side, a big feather pillow at the headboard with the imprint of his profile still carved in it; another pillow lay sideways on the left side of the mattress, and the fitted sheet, loose at one corner, still held the wrinkled impression of Gordon's hips.

On the painted wicker corner shelf there were two ashtrays, both overflowing with hollow filters, and there was another on the night table beside Gordon's bed, equally full. The trail of ashes strewn along the faded lime carpet between the bed and the desk reminded me of the breadcrumbs that Hansel and Gretel had left in the forest to find their way home, and for an odd moment the fanciful thought that there might have been some method to Gordon's careless smoking crept in at the back of my mind.

My search for something to seal the last packing crate was brief—cut short by the discovery of the matchbook, which I found in the little drawer of Gordon's bedside table. In all likelihood it wouldn't have grabbed my attention, were it not for its immaculate appearance amidst all of the dusty clutter in the drawer—that, and the fact that it was resting on top of the clutter, as if someone had recently placed it there, with the express intent that it would be found.

It was black and glossy, and it winked at me under the muted light of the bedside lamp's smoke-yellowed shade. It came out of the drawer between my fingers, its cover pristine, its rank and file of sulfur-tipped paper sticks all present and accounted for, its striking board unused.

I turned it over and flipped up the cover.

The foreign print on the inside flap didn't surprise me. Gordon often wrote reminders and notes to himself in one of the five languages in which he was fluent ("in case prying eyes should come across them," he once said with a curious smile—though there was no trace of humor in his pale blue eyes). He was a private and solitary man who counted those closest to him as mere acquaintances and those not so close as simply passersby. By his own admission, Gordon did not have conversations but rather mutually beneficial exchanges. To the best of my knowledge, I am the only fellow educator at West High that he had ever shared casual words with over a cup of coffee—and even those words seemed to carry a less than casual air. Gordon once referred to himself as the "personification of an enigma," and the glossy black matchbook with the code-like writing on its inside flap seemed to confirm the fact that he was determined to keep it that way. Even in death.

Still, the symbols inside the matchbook intrigued me, as did the strangely beautiful painting of the captive teenager, and later that night in the comfort of my own bed I dreamt that I was still in Gordon's apartment sorting through his things.

In the dream, Gordon was there helping me, and as the two of us worked side by side, stacking an endless supply of paintings into a makeshift staircase that climbed into the dark sky above his roofless apartment, he whistled Pearl Jam's *Nothing As It Seems*. There was nothing odd about his choice of tune—unlike a lot of older teachers, Gordon actually liked alternative rock. He just wasn't the sort of man who whistled while working.

As we continued to stack the paintings higher and higher into the night sky, I asked him what we were doing.

He stopped whistling just long enough to say: "Keeping these fucking things as far out of that asshole's reach as possible. Do you have the canvas?"

I nodded, a long and slow dream nod, as if my head were the size and weight of a hot air balloon, even though I had no idea what he was referring to.

He shouted at me over the stillness of the night air as if we were climbing a mountain in the middle of a wind storm: "Good! Keep it close! We're almost there!"

I nodded again, suddenly aware of the cold temperature at our advanced altitude. Cloud wisps swirled up my nose and caught in my throat like cotton.

"Breathe through your eyes!" Gordon shouted as he continued to stack paintings some four hundred feet above me. "It's the only way to survive at this altitude!"

I tried to cough, but no sound came out, and Gordon was screaming: "Fuck the swallows! They're filthy disease carriers, like the rest of the birds! Breathe with your eyes, man, or they'll tear out your lungs and use them for nesting!"

I opened my eyes, and the clouds were suddenly gone and fresh night air flooded my lungs, and Gordon was laughing like a half-crazed apparition of St. Nicholas from his spot on the summit above me. A hollow-point was clamped between his yellowed teeth, a black matchbook between the fingers of his right hand, a single match in his left, poised against the matchbook's little black striking board.

"I told you, Jack! The swallows! Fuck 'em! Anybody can swallow! Climb up here, and bring the canvas with you before that limp dick figures out he's been had!"

I started to climb again when something twinkled in the distance, a bright and luminescent something radiating from the dark side of the moon.

I looked up to find my former student, Mickey Greenleaf, perched comfortably on the lower curve of the quarter moon, his eyes dreamy yet fully alert as he bit into a big red apple.

For a moment I was nonplussed, unable to tell if the twinkling that had caught my eye was from the shine off of the apple or the brilliance of Mickey's sparkling teeth. He winked at me from his perch on the moon and smiled a big healthy *I'm-so-cute-and-you-know-it* smile, the sort of smile you just couldn't help but return. His eyes were as bright and blue as I'd remembered—their brilliant luster as blinding as it had been back in the day when he would gaze at me from the front row of my drama class during his senior year. And his silky blond bangs hung as always in delightful disarray. He was clad only in a crisp white pair of boxers, and as the toes of one bare foot stroked lazily at the sea of stars below him, I felt an almost painful surge of nostalgia.

When I raised a hand to wave to him, Gordon shouted from somewhere not so far above: "There will be plenty of time for that later, Jack! Don't let the destination decide the path! Many byways and shortcuts! The boy is an apple-polisher—fuck him!"

From his perch on the lower curve of the moon, Mickey grinned, as if he found the ranting old man at the top of the stack of paintings a mildly amusing joke. He took another bite out of his apple, and fresh juice dripped down his chin.

He winked at me again, as if we were both in on the joke. The dream became fragmented here, but it didn't matter; its essence had already broken free of my subconscious by that point.

When I returned to Gordon's apartment the following morning, I had come to a decision and cemented it by withholding the haunting fresco of the boy in bondage and taking only the five crated paintings to the local post office. I shipped them to Portsmouth with this note:

> *Dear Dr. Powell:*
> *Enclosed please find five paintings from your brother's collection—two Dalis, one Munch, one Gauguin, as well as an oil by Ivan Duprez. Though I have never heard of Mr. Duprez or his work (and I must confess, my knowledge of art is limited), I have included this painting with the others just in case it should turn out to be of value. If you can think of any other paintings in Gordon's collection that would be of interest to you, please let me know, and I will ship them to you at once.*
>
> *Sincerely,*
> *Jack McGregor*
> *3434 Tall Cedar Road*
> *Canaima, Pennsylvania 10090*

A little over a week later, I received one of the five crates I'd shipped to Portsmouth, along with this note:

> *Dear Mr. McGregor:*
> *Thank you for your prompt attention to the matter of the artwork I requested. Enclosed please find the oil by Duprez. Though I appreciate your effort, I have no interest in this particular piece. As with*

the rest of Gordon's paintings, you may dispose of the Duprez as you see fit.

Most Cordially,
Arthur C. Powell

Just like that, along with a fat cashier's check that more than covered my cost of shipping the five paintings to him. *Most* cordially, and no Ph.D. after his name this time. I was beginning to wonder if maybe Gordon's cold fish of an older brother was warming up to me when I noticed this postscript at the bottom of the page:

The enclosed painting was done by my brother; Duprez was a pseudonym he'd adopted while working at a Chicago art gallery—I can't recall which—several long decades past. I hope this information will be of value to you.

chapter two

another dream/the matchbook/snap decision

It would have ended right there, if not for the subsequent dream I had a few nights later—a sequel, of sorts, to the "staircase of paintings" dream.

I admit that Arthur Powell's last letter had intrigued me, and it certainly raised a perplexing question: If the Duprez I had shipped to him (as well as the one I'd kept—that paradoxically beautiful yet disturbing fresco of the boy in bondage) had in fact been painted by Gordon, why was there an entry in Gordon's ledger stating the value of both paintings as if he, Gordon, had purchased them? Had he sold them years ago and only recently bought them back, perhaps at a lower price than the purchaser had put out for them? I'd heard of such scams in the art world, and though I have no working concept of their machinations, I do know that a handful of less than reputable dealers have made small fortunes this way. Or had the paintings been sold by mistake and the fees in the ledger simply the price Gordon had to pay to get them back?

The solution to this little mystery would present itself later—under less pleasant circumstances—opening doorways to other questions whose answers would have a far greater impact than a simple art scam. But for now, the chain of ownership of the two paintings seemed nothing more than yet another curiosity in the chain of curiosities that wove throughout Gordon's life and afterlife.

The second dream I had was more revealing than the first. Indeed it was this dream that drove me beyond the point of intrigue and into the realm of possibility . . .

I was back on the staircase of paintings, seemingly miles above Gordon's tiny apartment building. I stood alone, barefoot and shirtless, clad only in a pair of jeans. My hair was wet, and my chest and shoulders were dappled with beads of moisture, as if I'd just stepped from the shower. The stars were gone from the sky, and thick banks of clouds passed by in eerie slow motion. Not far above me, the stacked paintings disappeared into the fluffy grey-edged whiteness of a huge slumbering thundercloud. Off to the left, the moon hung like a dull silver sliver, its dark side having swallowed most of the light, its lower curve unoccupied.

I opened my mouth as if to call out into the darkness when a facile hand landed on my shoulder. I turned to see Gordon standing behind me. He was dressed in a long white robe that looked more like it came from the Hilton than Heaven, but with his grey hair and spotty beard, it completed the ecumenical motif just the same. He leaned forward from the step above, a sinewy and liver-spotted forefinger pressed to his lips in a shushing gesture, and nodded in the general direction of a nearby passing cloud.

On the cloud, still clad in his white boxers, Mickey Greenleaf lay curled into a fetal position with his eyes closed and the thumb of his right hand tucked sweetly into his mouth. My heart did a sad somersault at the sight of him, and my knees nearly buckled. I was brought back to the purpose of the dream by Gordon's bony grasp on my shoulder.

When I turned to face him, he was standing a good three feet away, a hollow-point clamped between his teeth and, just as in the previous dream, a single match poised over the striking board of the black matchbook I'd found in his night table drawer.

He spoke to me in an exaggerated whisper, his pale blue eyes like faded denim set within the dark recesses of their sockets: "We're almost there, Jack. Do you have the canvas?"

I wanted to look back at Mickey—just to make sure that he was safe on his cloud, I told myself—but Gordon's haunted eyes held me motionless on the precipice of paintings. I wanted to answer him—felt compelled to do so—but my throat had locked in an unshakable death-grip, and my lips could manage scarcely more than a silent quiver. I was a kid again, in the presence of a forbidding authority figure: a *teacher*, with a blank test sheet in his hand, and me with no ready explanation for my lack of knowledge. I would have swallowed had I been able to produce the requisite amount of spit.

Gordon smiled at me then, a cunning yet benign smile. He chuckled softly and struck the match, long and slow, against the back of the matchbook. As he cupped the flame and brought it close to the tip of his cigarette, a brief glimpse of the tiny holographic letters embedded in the glossy black surface of the matchbook was revealed under its wavering glow. Then as the match was extinguished by the thin stream of smoke he exhaled over its tip, the silvery letters disappeared like the rabbit in a smoothly executed magic trick.

I turned at the sudden sound of thunder in the not too distant dark, only to find that Mickey's cloud had disappeared. I could hear Gordon coughing behind me, and from somewhere down below the muted howl of a wolf (or perhaps it was just a stray dog) rising on the gyrating wind that circled the staircase of paintings like an invisible serpent winding its way into an unbreakable stranglehold.

I woke with a jolt, the sheets tangled around my waist and legs, my half-asleep arms trapped under my body, my chest slick with sweat. Somewhere outside my open bedroom window the muted sound of thunder rumbled in the distance like a sleeping dinosaur, but the storm it threatened to presage never came.

By noon the following day, the sun reflected dazzling rays along the surface of the pond across the road from my apartment building, and there was scarcely a cloud in the sky. It was Saturday, and I was halfway through my workout when fragments of the dream I'd had the night before came back to me in a series of tableaux, like pictures in a flip-book that create the illusion of movement when you fan through them at a rapid pace. Out of all these stilted images, one caught my attention firmly enough to make me stop in the middle of a particularly productive ab-crunching session. I dangled upside down, my bent knees hooked around the sturdy bar that was fastened to the ceiling joists, my sweaty hair hanging toward the floor, my heart knocking a steady beat inside my chest, and I closed my eyes.

The image from the dream was clear as it played out against the dark screen of my eyelids and offered more than sufficient motivation. I curled upward one last time, scarcely feeling the burn in my stomach now as I grasped the overhead bar and pulled my legs free.

I found what I was looking for on my dresser. The matchbook I'd taken from Gordon's apartment. Shiny and black but otherwise nondescript. I took it to the window where the sun was shining in and turned it slowly from side to side in the light. It winked at me, just as it had the night I'd discovered it in the little drawer of Gordon's bedside table. Only this time I could see the discreet holographic print on its glossy surface. It read:

The Black Otter—Lounge and Extremities.

I gazed at the heading for a long moment, studying its concealed silver letters and the perplexing categorization on the other side of the dash—the same which brought a tingle to some distant and uncharted place inside of me:

Lounge and Extremities.

Looking at these words made me want something I hadn't had (nor felt the desire for) since I was a teenager: a cigarette. Not one of Gordon's hollow-points, either, but a Marlboro Red. Or a Winston.

I pushed back the sudden craving and concentrated on the matchbook; closer examination revealed an address in even smaller print at the bottom, but no phone number. But that didn't matter; the address was all I needed. I finished my workout and then went for a longer than average bike ride to make up for the one I'd missed out on the week before when I'd spent the entire weekend clearing out Gordon's office at the school and sorting through the paintings at his apartment. I got back to my apartment sometime after 5:00 P.M., and by 6:00 I was showered and dressed and on the road, headed north for The Black Otter.

The drive was pleasant, and I made good time, arriving at the Pierpoint county line in just over an hour. The early evening sky was a deep purple bruise spreading out across the western horizon as I followed the long and winding tree-lined road to the Gothic-looking structure at the top of the hill. The freshly mown lawn was expansive and bordered by thick green growth at its farthest edges. There were topiary animals strategically positioned like sentinels on either side of the old brown brick building. Clear water rippled gently in the pond that the cobblestoned drive circled in a broad arc. Ambient light spilled from recessed fixtures, illuminating the ornate archway of the main entrance.

A valet dressed in black trousers and a crisp white tunic stepped up to the curb as I brought the car to a stop. He was young, no more than eighteen. With his slicked back hair, sharp eyes, and flawless complexion, he looked as if he'd just stepped from the pages of a Fitzgerald novel. His smile was polite but genuine; his teeth were like a glowing advertisement for dental hygiene. Instead of giving me a ticket for my keys, he placed a glossy black card in my hand with an emblem on one side that was identical to the first Greek symbol that had been printed on the inside flap of the matchbook. I tipped him and headed up the dark slate steps.

At the huge oak door, I turned back (for what, I'm not quite sure) but my car and the valet were already gone.

Standing on the flagstone of the wide porch, I scarcely had enough time to second-guess my snap decision to come here when the door swept open, and a tall man in a white dinner jacket and black tie gestured toward the foyer. Like the valet, he was handsome and well-groomed, and about him there lingered the faint scent of a pleasant cologne. Pinned to the left lapel of his jacket was a red rose whose crisp petals had yet to unfold; affixed to the other lapel was a white gold Omega pin, which caught the minimal light in the entryway and twinkled briefly as he bowed. He was perhaps two years younger than I, with shoulders the width of goal posts and eyes like black pearls. As I passed through the foyer and stepped into the lobby, the sound of an unseen clock ticked away the seconds before the door swung shut behind me.

chapter three

the lobby/the bar/circumlocution

The lobby was considerably smaller than I'd imagined it would be—cozy, with the sound of snapping knots in the circular stone fireplace at its center. But the elegance of its decor made me feel uncomfortably underdressed. As if he could read my thoughts, the doorman smiled politely and said: "This way, sir, if you would, please."

He led me down a short corridor just beyond the front desk and into a small room that resembled the walk-in closet of a privileged gentleman. A single light burned from the recessed fixture at the center of the ceiling, casting its soft glow over the maple walls and olive carpeting. Dozens of freshly pressed suit jackets hung in neat rows on either side of the room, each draped with a clear plastic dust cover. Against the back wall there stood a tall cherry wood wardrobe with its double doors opened to reveal shelves of ties and handkerchiefs, like an elegant display in a posh men's shop.

The doorman selected a jacket from the rack on the left, removed its shiny dust cover, and held it out for me.

For a ridiculous half-second, I almost expected him to say, "Perhaps you would feel more comfortable in this, sir." When he said nothing, I turned and slipped my arms into the sleeves of the jacket, which fit perfectly.

I watched, still a little bemused, as he selected a tie from the top shelf of the wardrobe. Before I could say a word, he flipped the collar of my shirt up, slipped the tie around my neck and knotted it the way my mother used to when I was a teenager. When he finished, he turned my collar back down and dusted the jacket with a lint brush.

My stomach growled faintly, and I shifted from one foot to the other in a vain attempt to head off another attack. I hadn't eaten since noon, and it was already a quarter past 7:00. The doorman looked into my eyes with such naked passivity that my cheeks burned.

"Would you care for a refreshment, sir?"

I nodded, suddenly feeling parched as well as hungry. He led me to the lounge just off the lobby.

There were tables and chairs and, of course, a bar, but no waiters or waitresses. At least none in sight. On each of the twenty-odd tables was laid a tray of *hors d'oeuvres* that smelled as good as they looked (and tasted even better) along with a bottle of spring water chilling in a silver decanter, and fine crystal glassware. At the bar, there were other drinks to be had—from every imaginable brand of juice and flavored tonic water to the finest coffees and teas. Everything *but* alcoholic beverages.

The bartender, who looked like he could have been the valet's older brother, poured me a glass of tonic, with a twist of lime, and offered a fresh tray of *hors d'oeuvres*. There were others in the lounge—some sitting in groups, some in pairs, some alone, all of them male. Music drifted from unseen speakers, enveloping the lounge without overwhelming it. Though an occasional ear-blaster by *Rammstein* or *Tool* might be heard, for the most part, dark and slow tunes that lulled the listener into a nice little chill dominated the charts at The Black Otter's tea-totaling bar. Right now Mazzy Starr's *Fade Into You* was making its ghostly rounds under the soft buzz of near-whispered conversations.

I sat at the bar, sipping my tonic and observing the other patrons as unobtrusively as possible, while my thoughts drifted back to the matchbook that had brought me here, its slick black surface with the hidden emblem on the back cover. And that strange phrase beneath the name of the establishment. I had discovered the *Lounge* and now found myself more curious than ever about the *Extremities.*

Mazzy's *Fade* gave way to Blur's *Death of the Party* when nature called, and I got up to look for the facilities. I left a tip in the glass on the bar and finished off my tonic in a single gulp.

As I turned away and headed for the lobby, the bartender called out to me, and for an absurd second I thought he'd asked if I was looking for a room. It took a moment for my confusion to pass; then it hit me: the *rest*room. I nodded and said yes. He handed me a shiny black card, just like the one the valet had given me in exchange for my car keys, and told me to take it to the front desk in the lobby. I was halfway there when a smile that I couldn't suppress crept across my lips. *Not only do we validate for parking,* a voice in my head chimed in, *we also validate for pissing.*

There was no one at the front desk, and for a second I was tempted to tap the little silver bell on the leather blotter. I looked around for the doorman instead, but he was nowhere to be found. I studied the ornate moldings over the foyer's archway, the painting on the curved ceiling—an exquisite mini knockoff of the Sistine Chapel. From where I stood, the arched tunnel of the foyer, with its shiny brass gates standing open, looked like the stubby throat of some mythical creature, and a tiny irrational tendril of trepidation raced the curve of my spine as it suddenly occurred to me that this was what the throat would look like from the *inside.*

I took a step toward those gleaming gates, part of my mind convinced that at any moment they would clang shut like a set of teeth, closing off my only exit. Or maybe they would wait for me to get closer—within biting range.

At some remote corner of my mind, I began to gauge the distance between the front desk and the door, calculating the time it would take to clear the gates before . . .

Before what? Before the gates could chew me up and spit my remains down the stubby throat and back into the belly of The Black Otter for digestion?

I laughed out loud, a strange and mirthless sound that echoed off the domed ceiling, and the nape of my neck suddenly bristled with gooseflesh.

I could not remember ever having felt so completely alone—not as a child, not as an adult, not even when I was going through Gordon's personal effects at his dark little one-bedroom apartment on Jackson Street. But that was because in Gordon's apartment I really hadn't been alone. Gordon had left things for me there. Things to keep me company in his absence. Things to challenge my brain, the way Gordon himself always had. Puzzles with white pieces. Strange riddles involving naked boys, bound and blindfolded. Cryptic clues, hidden on the covers and inside flaps of matchbooks. A trail of ashes. An unflappable older brother. Greek symbols and pseudonyms. All part of his plan to . . .

To what? Lead me eighty miles up north to the Gothic house on the hill where all his secrets would be revealed—secrets his brother and everyone else who knew him, myself included, never suspected? Was I here to bear witness to the revelation that Gordon could not have brought himself to unveil in life? Was I his lone apostle carrying paintings into the night sky where teenage boys slept on clouds and dipped their toes into a sea of stars while reclining on the lower curve of a quarter moon?

Or was I here for another reason?

My cheeks burned as thoughts of that eerily beautiful painting resurfaced. I closed my eyes, and a sudden, almost overwhelming surge of nostalgia shot through me like vertigo. A lost image, randomly selected from my memory, barely cohesive, more of a feeling actually, melding with the image of the naked boy in bondage created by Duprez, aka Gordon Powell.

I clenched my teeth and shook my head hard and fast enough to crack my neck, and the image vanished.

I turned back to the desk. The young man standing there looked up as if I'd just arrived and he had never left. His short blond hair was spiked and shiny, and his grey-green eyes smiled even when his mouth wasn't in on the act. He was dressed like the doorman, complete with the Omega pin on his lapel. He couldn't have been more than twenty-two.

His dimples made such a stunning appearance when he asked "How may I be of assistance, sir?" that I almost forgot what I'd come for. Some part of my brain that was still functioning sent the signal to my hand, and I placed the glossy black card on the blotter before him.

He took the card and made it disappear under the desk, without giving it as much as a cursory glance. Then he placed a leather binder on the blotter and opened it to the first page. There were twenty-four 5 x 7 black glossy sheets inside, each embossed with a letter of the Greek alphabet. I stopped at sigma, not needing to retrieve the matchbook from my pocket to compare the symbol on its inside flap. The letter on the eighteenth page of the leather binder was the same.

When I looked up at the desk clerk, his mouth joined his eyes in completing the smile.

"Excellent choice, sir," he said. The glare of his teeth was nearly blinding. I concentrated on his eyes, but it wasn't much easier. He said something else, but I couldn't hear it over the steady hum of his eyes. I felt a distant pressure in my kidneys and vaguely remembered having to go to the bathroom.

I snapped back to myself when he repeated the question: "Will you be requiring any extrapolative accoutrements?"

I had no idea what he meant so I shook my head. His short smile made me feel naked; I could feel the warmth returning to my cheeks, but it was impossible to look away from him. He turned to the computer screen and clicked the mouse twice.

"Will this be cash, charge, or check?"

My bank card was in my wallet, but I didn't want to use it unless I had to. I didn't want to give him my name, but unless the cost of the Sigma was ninety-seven dollars or less, I had no choice—short of changing my mind and heading for the door.

I cleared my throat and asked, "How much?"

He smiled again, as if he'd just remembered an amusing anecdote, and the tie that the doorman had put around my neck suddenly seemed to tighten. I had to force myself not to tug at my collar. My heart sounded like a huge hammer in my chest. The desk clerk was typing again when I felt the cold finger of panic touch my spine. I reached for my wallet and was about to say "credit" when his smile was replaced by a frown.

"I'm afraid the Sigma is already taken this evening, sir," he said, without looking up from the screen. The area behind the desk was even more dimly lit than the lobby, and the computer cast a soft blue glow against his profile, accentuating his cheekbones and dimples. As I stood with my wallet still in hand, I began to wonder what the chief prerequisite was for employment at The Black Otter. Did the management simply flip through the pages of the latest Abercrombie & Fitch catalogue? Or did they recruit cocky little apple-polishers straight out of the local high schools and colleges?

"However," the desk clerk continued, his eyes still on the computer screen, "if you would be interested in the viewing room . . . "

"Excuse me?"

"If you'd like, I could inquire as to its availability, sir."

He looked directly into my eyes, and suddenly for the life of me I could not remember why I had come here in the first place—the pain in my kidneys had mysteriously receded, and I was beginning to feel a little foolish.

I nodded and croaked out something like "yes, please," which made me feel worse than foolish: it made me feel weak.

I cleared my throat, more loudly than necessary, and straightened my back, but the clerk took no notice. His fingers machine-gunned over the keyboard, and momentarily the computer emitted a short beep. He picked up the phone and dialed three digits.

"Yes, this is Devon at the front desk. I have a gentleman here who's interested in the Sigma's viewing room this evening. Would your party have any objections or exceptions? . . . Standard discount . . . No sir, the gentleman has nothing to declare . . . Special restrictions apply, yes sir." He listened for a moment; then without offering me as much as a side glance, he said: "Mid- to late-twenties, brown and blue, five-eleven, one seventy-five, ten to twelve BFP, athletic, Gaelic descent, no facial scarring, no visible tattoos or piercings . . . Very good, sir, thank you." He hung up the phone, and his smile made a winning comeback.

The standard discount came to ninety dollars even, so my card remained in my wallet.

I rode what appeared to be the establishment's sole elevator down to the basement level with seven dollars in my pocket, a line of sweat running down my back, and a swarm of butterflies beating at the wall of my stomach like a phantom flock of swallows from some old horror story I'd read back in high school.

The elevator car swooped in what felt like an endless subterranean descent, and my stomach rose, adding to the growing sensation of vertigo within. My mind was racing, trying to process everything that had happened so far—this strange place; the haunting painting that had brought me here; the supercilious yet ingratiating smile of the desk clerk, Devon, and the way he'd hit my personal information spot-on (right down to what I presume was my body fat percentage—"ten to twelve BFP"), with scarcely a glance. What any of that information could possibly have to do with anything, I couldn't begin to guess. And just what the hell were the "special restrictions" that applied to me?

The elevator doors opened on a hallway that looked like the starting point of a particularly intricate maze. The black tiled floor glistened as if still wet from the mop. The recessed ceiling fixtures bounced circles of dim light against the shiny floor every ten paces or so, like halos. The walls looked to be made of some monochromatic material; nothing like what you'd expect to find in the lower levels of an old mansion like The Black Otter. Inside the overhead ductwork, regulated air whispered in a steady stream as if Zeus himself were exhaling one long final breath.

I stepped into the corridor, and as the elevator doors slid shut behind me, the lights flickered briefly and a door opened on my left. The young man who greeted me had a smile so bright it nearly put Devon's to shame. His hair was combed back, but without the aid of mousse or gel, so when he greeted me with a cordial nod the bangs spilled over his forehead, making him look all of eighteen. Without warning a cool voice inside my head whispered: *Apple-polisher.*

For a moment I found it hard to breathe. I felt as if somehow the elevator had taken me through a porthole in time and that I was five years in the past, staring at my former student Mickey Greenleaf. The hair, the eyes, the mouth, the nose—right down to the rounded shoulders and prominent chest of a boy who easily could have been an Olympic gymnast, had he so desired.

As we passed under the first circle of light, the illusion was broken, but still the urge to brush his bangs back out of his eyes was strong enough to make me shove my hands deep into the pockets of my trousers.

After a series of maze turns, which Mickey's at-a-glance double navigated with the sure foot of a seasoned tour guide, we reached a door that blended into the wall so well that at first I'd thought he'd lost his way. The blood at my temples struck a dull yet steady series of blows as I waited for him to make the next move—open the door, press a buzzer, knock, whatever protocol dictated in a place like this. But he just stood there, patiently waiting, with a mixture of confidence an innocence that was mildly unnerving.

I studied him under the light that fell across the doorway, and in spite of the way his upper body filled out the crisp white shirt he wore, I suddenly found myself wondering how I could have ever thought he looked like an eighteen-year-old. Surely he couldn't have been any older than fifteen, sixteen at the most. His cheeks had a healthy pink hue and his lips looked as though they'd never been kissed.

Slow seconds passed as we waited outside the door, the two of us, face to face.

He looked at me with a candor that bordered insolence, but I held my gaze as my heart slammed slow in my chest. I was a teacher and I would be damned if I was going to let someone young enough to be in my charge put a spook on me. His gaze intensified and I nearly blinked under the pressure. I smiled instead, a speculative smile that I'd used with countless students before, and made the one move he would not be anticipating.

I asked him his age.

He smiled as if I'd goosed him and his cheeks went two shades pinker. But his gaze didn't waver—to the contrary, it intensified, as if to reaffirm the parameters of decorum and proper employee-customer etiquette, as if to say: *My resolve is as hard as my body and you'll need more than a cheap come on like that to break it, Teach.*

In a lucid flash, I could see myself shoving him against the wall and slapping that condescending smirk right off his unkissed lips. In my mind's eye I could see this as a long overdue act of retribution—a sudden act of violence justified by the very nature of the victim, a punishment that may not fit the crime but nonetheless one that would produce the desired response: humility.

When I came back to myself, I saw that he was still standing before me, unmolested. As I looked into his eyes, I felt that something needed to be said—just what, I didn't know—but before I could speak, the door we were standing in front of opened and the evening-attired man who'd greeted me in the lobby upstairs (he of the broad shoulders and black pearl eyes) said: "This way, if you please, sir. We've been waiting for you."

I looked back at the boy. His bangs were still in his eyes, but the smarmy smile was gone. In its place there was an expression of solemn subordination, that of a dutiful pupil who would freely offer his head to the chopping block if it so much as obstructed his teacher's view of the blackboard.

As I passed through the doorway into the viewing room, I was grateful that he hadn't told me his age, and even more grateful that I didn't know his name.

chapter four

the viewing room/the sigma/come together

THERE WAS A SOFT CLICK AS THE DOOR CLOSED BEHIND ME, cutting off the minimal light from the outside hallway. This was followed by a brief moment of complete darkness before a cool blue spotlight fell over the only seat in the room. The chair was suspended from the ceiling like the seat of an inverted roller coaster. But it wasn't made of hard plastic. Thickly padded, with a plush leather covering, right down to its shoulder harness and armrests, it looked comfortable enough to fall asleep in. Closer examination of the chair revealed a leather-wrapped joystick on the right armrest and a four-button keypad on the left. The chair's sturdy support rod disappeared somewhere in the blackness overhead, where the machinery that actually propelled the "ride" was concealed as well. The shoulder harness stood in its upright position. The glass window directly opposite the chair held a shadowy reflection of the rest of the room. I could see myself in its flawless curved surface—first standing beside the chair; then sitting in it, my legs dangling inches from the ground.

The doorman appeared from the shadows behind me

and brought the shoulder harness down over my chest. Its metal tab locked into place at the fork of my thighs. The harness was snug but comfortable. I looked at my reflection in the darkened pane of glass again and wondered if possibly I'd gotten myself in over my head. Then something clanged in the machinery overhead, and the chair suddenly felt as if it were floating. I took in a breath and didn't let it out. A sound like an air conditioning unit kicking in came from the darkness above, and I had to knuckle under to keep my eyes from shutting tight.

When the chair swayed a little to the left, I let out the breath I was holding—just enough to open my mouth and speak. I have no idea exactly what I was going to say, but I knew that I wanted whatever this was to stop right here. I suddenly had no desire to probe the secrets of The Black Otter. I no longer cared about the mystery boy in the painting, the code on the matchbook—and much less, what lay beyond that curved pane of glass. I only wanted off this ride as quickly as possible. They could keep my money and have a good laugh over the chickenshit who couldn't even handle the viewing room. I just wanted this to end right here and now.

I was about to announce my desire to back out when the doorman spoke softly yet clearly from someplace behind me.

"The controls are completely at your disposal, sir."

He explained that "the stick" on my right armrest would move the chair forward, backward, and to either side, covering the 180° angle of the glass for my "enhanced viewing pleasure." The buttons on the left armrest, he added, controlled the height and angle of the chair. The pull tab encircled by these buttons was to be used only in the event that I needed the viewing to stop ("for whatever reason, do not hesitate"), at which point the semicircular glass observation window would go dark, the blue center spot would resume, and the chair would automatically return to its starting position, where the harness would release and I would be free to exit the room.

To this, he offered one caveat: "Once the center tab is pulled, the viewing is over. There is no way to reset the chamber, so please use it only in the event of a personal emergency." He paused and added: "Understand that you cannot affect the outcome of the actions performed in the Sigma Room. You are merely an observer, and participation is strictly forbidden. No cameras or recording devices are allowed in the viewing rooms. The glass is a one-way mirror, and your privacy is guaranteed. Do you have any questions, sir?"

I shook my head, where things were rapidly changing. My eyes were now glued to the darkened pane of glass before me, my reflection therein.

"Do you have any requirements at this time, sir?"

I shook my head again.

"Has everything been explained to your complete satisfaction?"

I nodded.

"Then, sir, I wish you a pleasurable journey into the soul of The Sigma," he said, and instantly the blue spotlight was extinguished.

In the complete and sudden darkness that followed, the soft click of the closing door echoed like a coin hitting the flat surface of a tin plate at the bottom of a deep well, and I found myself holding my breath for the second time that evening.

I don't recall the exact moment I released this breath. It could have been when the microphone inside the Sigma room was turned on (and the sound of movement in the darkness beyond the one-way glass came through the speakers mounted somewhere above me). Or when the velvet drapes surrounding the glass from the inside separated like the curtains at a playhouse or a cinema. It could have been, in the subsequent seconds, when the jukebox at the far left side of the Sigma glowed into eerie yet soundless life, all bluish-green, with a splash of pink. Or maybe it was when the spotlight mounted to the right corner of the windowless rear wall filled the lower left area of the Sigma with a soft blue light that was at once both ambient and cold.

In truth, I don't remember breathing at all. The only function I remember with total clarity is the strong and steady pulse of blood at my temples—that, coupled with the earsplitting double shutter-click of each blink of my eyes, was the only reason I had to believe that I was fully awake and not dreaming . . . and further, that I was in fact still drawing breath and very much alive.

Beyond the one-way glass, a tall guy in his mid- to late-twenties stood at the jukebox. Dressed in business attire—a dark suit, with a red silk tie and matching handkerchief poking artfully out of the breast pocket—he was lean and somewhat hungry looking. His features were sharp and angular, leaning toward the aristocratic. His narrow lips were paradoxically voluptuous, and his pale blue eyes appeared at once both alert and remote. His shoulder-length auburn hair was tied back into a ponytail by a thin black ribbon, which was knotted in a simple bow at the back of his head. A stray lock of hair fell over his left eye and curled into a loose question mark just below his dimpled chin.

The jukebox must have had a delay mechanism because the music didn't start playing until after he'd entered the last of several selections on its keypad. The first sound rose from the speakers in a single note that hung on the air for an indeterminable length of time. As the soft blue-green ornamental light from the jukebox glowed against the ponytailed man's regal profile, that single note gave way to an instrumental piece, vaguely familiar, low and undulating, underscoring the following movements with uncanny precision, as if the entire scene had been choreographed.

As the tall figure turned from the jukebox, the light

mounted to the upper left corner of the rear wall came on, bathing the right side of the room in that same cool yet cozy blue glow, and my focus shifted to the naked young man strapped to the slanted bench.

He looked the same as he had in the painting, his exceptional physique accentuated by the lighting, like an artist's rendering—only more *tangible.* As if to prove this, the tall guy with the ponytail stepped forward and casually ran his fingertips along the curve of the boy's right upper arm, which tensed, seemingly out of reflex, then relaxed as the fingers glided away.

I sat watching for a moment, incapable of movement, feeling the harness pressing against my chest like a tremendous weight.

Then I remembered the controls at my fingertips.

As the chair moved closer to the window, my mouth became dry, and my eyes felt wet and warm. I could hear the ponytailed guy breathing through his nose under the steady workings of the industrial music coming from the jukebox's speakers. Then his voice came clearly through the speakers mounted somewhere in the darkness above me, like a whisper filtered through a megaphone, a pleasant, almost soothing baritone. He was telling the naked young man strapped to the slanted bench that everything was all right, that he was going to be just fine; all he had to do was lie still and let it happen. He stroked the boy's hair with one hand while working the other up the sculpted curve of his inner thigh.

The boy's face was obscured by the oversized blindfold he wore, just as it had been in Gordon's painting. But his lips were exposed as if inviting a kiss, and the ponytailed guy placed a finger to them in a shushing gesture. Then slowly, the finger slid between those lips, and Ponytail instructed the boy to suck. The boy's acquiescence was tentative at first, then more aggressive, like an infant drawing sustenance. As the finger slid from the boy's mouth, his lips continued to work, and Ponytail soothed him by stroking his hair again while applying the saliva to his nipples as if it were a salve. The boy moaned once, and Ponytail shushed him, gently, soothingly.

Ponytail continued to stroke the boy's hair as he asked him how old he was. When the boy responded with a whispered "eighteen," Ponytail asked him if he was sure. "You look younger than that," he said. "Tell me the truth. I won't tell anyone. I promise."

The boy's mouth worked in that tentative way again, and secretly I found myself in awe of his talent. A subtle shift in his expression and suddenly he looked no older than sixteen. A dangerous age—one that could lead to all sorts of trouble for anyone whose eye he happened to catch, and he knew it. The image of a shiny green apple centered on a desk before the blackboard popped into my head, and I couldn't shake it. I understood the excitement that Ponytail was feeling. I recognized the danger that not only surfaced from this excitement but encircled it like an intoxicating vapor, an enchanted mist which only heightened the effect.

My hand worked the control on the armrest of the suspended seat, drawing me closer to the window, and when the boy said that he was sixteen, my heart did a somersault, despite the fact that I knew he was lying.

Ponytail stood and removed his jacket. There was nowhere to hang it, so he simply let it drop to the floor. He slipped out of his expensive shoes while he unbuttoned his shirt. His tasteful silk tie fell to the floor along with his shirt, and his crisply pleated trousers joined them shortly. He removed his socks in two smoothly executed movements.

Now he stood above the boy clad only in a pair of silk boxers that matched his tie, his body tight and toned. As he knelt, the muscles in his long thighs moved like well-oiled pistons. He brought his lips close to the boy's right ear.

"Is this your first time?" Though he spoke in a whisper, his voice came clearly through the speakers on my side of the curved glass wall.

When the boy nodded, my heart took another serious roll, even though I knew he was lying again. His performance was seamless, and judging by the way Ponytail was taking him in with his hungry eyes, I don't think it would have mattered to anyone within viewing distance but me.

"It's all right," Ponytail said. "Just lie still and do exactly what I say, do you understand?"

Again the boy nodded, his lips parted in perfect mimicry of his expression in the painting I'd found in Gordon's apartment.

I wanted to tell Ponytail to remove the blindfold so I could see the boy's eyes—so the *boy* could see *me* watching him, so that he would know that I knew how he'd spit-shined every apple he'd ever placed on a teacher's desk. I wanted the boy to know that Gordon hadn't taken the secret to his grave, that he had left a trail of ashes for me to follow to this place. I wanted him to look at me and know that I now knew what he *really* was. I wanted him to know that I was on to him, that there would be no more extended deadlines at the drop of a sweet smile, no more eleventh-hour reprieves at a well-practiced upward glance from under his tousled bangs. But not with that blindfold on. Because, in truth, I couldn't be sure. Not one hundred percent sure. Not until I could see his eyes.

The instrumental piece faded and a new song came from the jukebox's speakers. A cover of The Beatles' *Come Together* by Aerosmith.

As the familiar riff worked its way into me, Ponytail looked up at the one-way glass, and his pale eyes twinkled as if he could see right through it. I shifted slightly in the seat, my right hand hovering over the leather-wrapped joystick, in case I needed to make a hasty retreat.

Ponytail grinned, still looking at the mirrored glass as if he could see me strapped into the suspended chair beyond it. My middle finger gently brushed the rounded top of the joystick, nothing more.

Ponytail rose and approached the glass. Had the observation window not been between us, he could have reached out and touched me. As the line of cold sweat at my back spread out, my breath began to come in quick, short waves. And still I did not use the joystick.

Ponytail placed his hands on the glass above his head, as if testing it for weak spots. With his arms stretched above him, I could see the two thin strips of his underarm hair, which confirmed that he was in fact a natural redhead. The rest of his body was perfectly smooth. He began to stroke the glass to the beat of the music, caressing it lovingly with his fingertips . . . all the while staring at me as if he could see straight through the one-way glass, as if he were looking not into my eyes but my soul.

My hand continued to hover over the joystick, but it had become unsteady. He was toying with me, and it was working. He didn't know exactly where I was, but he sensed that I was close and knew that my eyes were on him. He was an exhibitionist (he would have never agreed to let me watch, otherwise—with or without the "special restrictions" that applied to me, whatever that meant) and he wanted the voyeur on the other side of the looking-glass to be as much a part of this as possible.

I told myself that it was nothing personal, that he was just trying to give me my money's worth by putting on a show. I told myself this again and again as I sat strapped into the suspended chair of the viewing room, the panic button the doorman had shown me about a million miles from my conscious thoughts.

He's just fucking with you, Jack. Don't let it get to you.

He smiled at me then and dropped a lascivious wink as if he could hear my thoughts, and I could see that one of his canines stood crooked in what otherwise would have been a perfect row of teeth. He tongued his crooked tooth in what was nothing more than a habitual gesture, but my throat tightened anyway.

When my gaze shifted back to his body, he began to flex for me—arms, chest, abs, forearms, biceps, triceps, the works—as if he *knew* that my gaze had shifted. Our eyes met again—but his were too anxious this time; they had moved too quickly, and the illusion that he could actually see me was broken.

He smiled again, but it came off more like the snarl of an animal. A sinewy timber wolf. His senses were exceptional. Either that or he was simply a good guesser. Or maybe this was all part of a routine that he had played out dozens of times before, and this was the moment where he would reveal his petulance over being "found out."

Whatever the case, he gazed at the glass with an expression of such raw insolence that, for a moment, he looked more like a teenager than the boy strapped to the bench behind him. Then his smile reappeared, confident, arrogant, and he was ten years older again. Just like that.

He dropped his silk boxers and took hold of his erection, which stood up straight, then hooked forward a few inches before the head. He looked down at it as he stroked it slowly to the beat of the music. In profile, he looked like a warrior preparing to reap the spoils of his army's latest conquest.

He continued to stroke himself, not caring whether or not I was watching anymore, knowing full well that I was. He looked up at me without missing a stroke. When he spoke, his voice sounded filtered as if through a tin can, and I assumed that this was because he was too close to the glass and just far enough out of the center microphone's range.

"You like to watch, don't you," he said softly. "It's OK. I like to be watched. That seat moves all over in there. You don't have to stay in one position. You can try it out right now if you want to while I'm doing this. Go ahead. I like to do this for a while before I get started." He tossed a nod toward the boy behind him. "It's not like he's going anywhere."

He continued to work his erection for about a minute or so in silence. I kept the chair where it was. I was unable to move. He stroked without looking at me—or his reflection in the glass, as it were—and I held my breath. Then suddenly the base of his closed fist hit the glass, the thumping sound it made filtered through the speakers but not through the glass. I jumped in my seat just the same. He was staring at me again, his nostrils flaring white.

"It's bulletproof," he said, as he continued stroking without missing a beat. "They don't want any . . . accidents, you know?"

He shook his head and smiled a small smile as if remembering a particularly humorless joke. His eyes looked nearly forlorn for a moment. Then he tossed his head back and let out a short chuckle. Then he leaned his forehead against the glass and rolled it slowly in my direction.

"Are you still there? Are you there, you *stealthy* little fuck? Are you watching me, little Scottish boy? Are you drooling over me? Or is it *him* you want?"

His snarling smile returned. He tongued his crooked tooth thoughtfully; then his smile became a knowing grin.

"If it's him you want, it's him you'll have. Tell you what I'm gonna do. I'm gonna go get some. You just stay there and watch while I go ball this kid. OK? You watch cos that's your job." He turned his head away. "You watch cos that's all you can do. But I'll tell you what—you're helpless. Don't even try to deny it, you know that you are. You're as helpless as he is. You're two fuckin buds in a bowl, and I'm gonna smoke your tight little muffin asses, Watcher. You got that? I'm gonna smoke his tight little ass, and all you can do is watch cos that's all you are is a fuckin watcher."

He moved away from the glass and went to the bench, where the boy lay like an offering, a sedated sacrifice. Then his voice came in a whisper, one which filtered through the speakers with perfect clarity now that he was back in range of the microphone.

"Watch watch watch, little Watcher . . . watch watch watch me smoke this sweet bitch's tight little ass for your vicarious pleasure . . . watch watch watch me and learn . . . "

I watched as Ponytail took a small bottle from the pocket of his coat and squirted a thin line of oil from the boy's chest to his navel. He set the bottle down without snapping the lid shut and began to work the oil into the boy's smooth skin, rubbing it over his chest and stomach. Then he did the boy's arms, rubbing down into his shaved armpits, along his sides, onto his buttocks, all the while telling the boy how hard and strong his body was and how good he was being—which was good, he warned, because if the boy was *bad* he would have to *punish* him, perhaps severely. "But," he added with a wink and grin, "You'd probably like that too much, wouldn't you?" He paused and added: "I'm sure the Watcher would."

By the time he'd finished oiling the boy's entire body, Aerosmith's *Come Together* had given way to Sarah McLachlin's *Building a Mystery*. For the next six songs, Ponytail stroked and tasted the boy, shifting his angle of approach every sixty seconds or so—save for a long exchange spent on his knees between the boy's spread legs, where his long and skillful tongue worked tirelessly for nearly an entire song (Marcy Playground's *Sex & Candy*).

Two songs later, when Ponytail was primed and ready to make full contact, Depeche Mode's *In Your Room* began to strike its first haunting chords.

As he slipped between the boy's legs and entered him, I closed my eyes. But still I could hear the sound of them. I could smell the sweat coming off of my body. I could feel the strength of my own erection pressing against the zipper of my jeans, and even though I was powerless to stop it, I loathed myself for it.

From the viewing room's speakers, I could hear Ponytail once again asking the boy "How old are you?" in a breathless and ragged voice, and the boy's response, broken by ever quickening thrusts. Sixteen, eighteen, whatever the guy sticking it to him wanted to hear. More questions—*Is this your first time? Do you like it? Does it feel good? Do you want me? Faster? Slower? Harder?*—to which the answer was always yes. The sound of Ponytail's lips kissing, his tongue lapping, the sweat-soaked smack of their bodies crashing together, and that recurring question: *How old are you? Say sixteen, say eighteen, say anything I want you to say, I'll be so gentle, so gentle, buddy, just tell me how old you are . . .*

Then finally Ponytail had stopped speaking, and there was a prolonged moaning sound mixed with a slew of incomprehensible syllables. Then the only sound coming from the speakers was that of labored breathing, winding down to a whisper in a well.

When I finally opened my eyes, Ponytail was wiping himself down with a towel by the jukebox, which now stood silent and dark. There was no sign of the sleek wolf about him anymore. Loose strands of his hair fell from his once tightly pinned tail. He looked spent.

I watched as he collected his clothes and left the Sigma by way of the concealed door on the back wall, without a word or a glance back at either the one-way glass or the boy on the slanted bench—apparently, he was finished with both of us. The door closed, disappearing into the wall, as if it had never existed.

I looked back at the bench and caught a quick glimpse of the boy still bound there before the lights went out and the curtain inside fell. The forefinger of my left hand was still wrapped tightly around the panic button's pull tab when the doorman came to show me out.

chapter five

moonlight mile/rufus/afterthoughts

I DROVE WITHOUT THINKING MOST OF THE WAY BACK, AND WHEN I saw the sign announcing *YOU ARE NOW ENTERING CANAIMA COUNTY—PLEASE DRIVE SAFELY,* I turned on the radio just in time to catch the 10:00 P.M. play of The Rolling Stone's *Moonlight Mile* on WNUK. The DJ, Dave Browne, was a former student of mine, and The Stone's *Moonlight Mile* was his signature piece; he never signed on without it.

I settled back into my seat, holding the wheel in one hand, letting the music carry me through, wishing I had something more in my stomach than just the *hors d'oeuvres* I'd consumed in the lounge at The Black Otter. I turned up the volume to elevate the good vibe over the bad one, and when Dave came on at the song's end to welcome his "one and a half listeners," a small smile curled at one corner of my mouth. When he was still my student, Dave had told me how he was going to be on the radio one day and that, even if nobody else tuned in, he'd always have one and a half listeners "because you always give me that extra fifty percent, Mr. M." I suppose that sounds pretty corny, but when you're a teacher fresh out of college, and you hear it coming from a seventeen-year-old student who only a year before was seriously considering dropping out of school, it's not too shabby.

As I listened to Dave's opening monologue, The Black Otter and the events of the past few weeks that had led up to my trip there this evening receded. I cracked the window, letting the night air flow in, like a current or a cooling wave, and felt the pressure in my head release in a single exhale. As I drove down the dark highway, past the surrounding farmlands, I listened to my former pupil cracking wise in his standard rapid-fire way about everything from politics to fashion. I actually laughed out loud at one point. But mostly I just smiled at the familiarity of this voice from the not-so-distant past coming through the speakers of my car.

By the time Dave had finished his opening monologue, and the first song of the first set of requests started to play, my stomach was growling. I took the next exit off the highway, but instead of turning east, the direction of my apartment, I headed west, toward the strip mall just past Highway 80.

The bistro was pleasantly lit with the sort of décor that invited laptops and books. There was a fireplace near the front window, comfortable chairs, and a bamboo coffee table, upon which an array of magazines were spread. Low-hanging lamps lit the tables along the wall opposite the main counter, creating the illusion of intimacy in a space far too narrow for any real privacy.

A familiar-looking girl took my order and smiled as she rang it up. When she noted that I was out late for a school night, I gathered that she was a graduate of West High, though I was fairly certain that she wasn't a former student of mine. Her name tag, which was hand-written in fluorescent green marker, read: KAITLIN. She said she was a senior in my first year at West High, and that her best friend Marilyn had been in my drama class. I nodded, not only because I remembered Marilyn, but because I now made the connection between Kaitlin's familiar-looking face and the past: she had briefly dated Mickey Greenleaf.

"I tried *so* hard to get into your drama class, but it was already full," she said. "That was a very depressing time, because every day I had to listen to either Mickey or Marilyn telling me what a cool class it was, and how cool Mr. M. was, and what a great time they were having . . . " She shook her head and laughed, a sweet laugh that seemed to have just a tinge of regret in it. No. Not regret. Bitterness. Then her eyes became sly, almost conspiratorial, and she grinned in a manner that was all too familiar to me. It was the grin a student gives a trusted teacher just before revealing a secret too delicious to keep. "You know that they were rivals over you," she said, pitching her voice low.

I furrowed my brow and gave an appropriate half-smile.

"Oh, *God*, yes!" she said, no longer bothering with the just-between-you-and-me whisper. "We used to call it The Mickey and Marilyn Smackdown when they'd start going at it. They would actually *fight* over you! Well, not *physically*, but you know what I mean."

I didn't. I had no idea what she meant. But I wanted to. I wanted her to elaborate on the whole thing, fill me in blow by blow, but I couldn't stand there like a teenager hungry for gossip. I had to remain casually, if somewhat quizzically, neutral. I smiled, hoping that my cheeks were appropriately flushing. I assumed that they were because Kaitlin was smiling right back at me in a way that indicated she was just as willing to dish it out as I was to spoon it up.

"I mean, look at you," she said, her eyes flaring. "You still look the same. Everyone thought you were a *student* that first day. My friend Hailee was in your first period English class, and she said that the class was like in shock when you came in and put your stuff on the teacher's desk. Everybody was talking about you at lunch!"

I could feel my cheeks burning this time. I'd heard of the student reaction to my arrival through the faculty grapevine. There had even been some discussion among a few teachers over whether my presence in the classroom might prove too much of a distraction for students to receive a proper education, and for a while it actually seemed as if the matter might come before the school board. Thankfully, Gordon had stepped in at an impromptu meeting of the disgruntled teachers in the lounge one afternoon. According to Caryl Folger, who had been present in the lounge when it all went down, the "gang of four" as she referred to them had been shut down when Gordon, sitting quietly in his usual spot and smoking one of his hollow-points, spoke up, softly yet decisively, and assured all present that the matter would not be brought up before the board. Caryl noted that a silence unlike any she had ever experienced followed Gordon's statement and that shortly thereafter the "gang of four" dispersed, leaving Gordon all by himself in the faculty lounge. If there ever had been further discussion on the matter between them, it certainly never came up at a school board meeting.

Kaitlin was smiling at me again, and telling me about her plans to go back to college and get her master's degree. I wanted to hear more about Mickey and Marilyn—specifically Mickey, considering what I'd seen at The Black Otter (or thought I'd seen—I still couldn't say with any certainty that the boy tied to the bench in the Sigma was in fact Mickey Greenleaf, or if he was just a guy who happened to look like Mickey). But it appeared that Kaitlin had crossed that bridge and was headed on to the greener pasture of her own future. For a moment I thought about taking a shot and asking her if she'd ever heard from Marilyn or Mickey after graduation, and if she knew what they were up to these days. But I just smiled and wished her well with her masters degree, and gave her my order.

When the bell dinged at the far end of the tall counter, which was stacked high with bread and rolls, I went to get my tray. My thoughts were still occupied with Mickey, and by extrapolation—however tenuous the thread—that peculiar establishment buried deep in the woods of Pierpoint. I was so deeply lost in thought that at first glance I failed to recognize the tall kid behind the counter who'd just set out my tray. Only adding to my confusion was the manner of his dress—the apron over his shirt, the backward turned ball cap, and the name tag that read: RUFUS. The smile on his face put me off, as well. Normally it took a lot of work to bring out that smile . . . or to even get him to peek out from the veil of his bangs. With his hair swept back under the ball cap and his face exposed, he looked like a completely different person. Happy. Almost confident.

"Hey, what's up?" I said. "I forgot that you work here."

He raised a clever brow and spoke in a tone of voice that at once sounded oddly foreign and completely natural to my ears. "I didn't know you *knew* that I worked here."

My immediate reaction to this heretofore unseen side of him must have put him off, because his expression shifted from slyly confident Rufus back to introverted Shane Guerin in an instant, as if a switch had been turned off inside him.

"I'm sorry," he said, his cheeks flushing a little.

"No, my bad," I said, and immediately his eyes were up at my unexpected and casual use of slang. "For a second there I thought you were a student of mine . . . Rufus, is it?"

A small smile crept at the corners of his mouth—he was a bright kid.

"You look just like him," I continued, now that I knew he was following me. "Dead ringer, in fact. Only he's much more reserved. Quiet sort of guy, very low key. A bit of a wallflower. Decent swimmer, though."

"Only decent?" Shane chimed in, raising a clever brow, and shifting easily back into "Rufus" mode.

"Well, he *could* shave a few seconds off of his 100-metre freestyle . . . "

"Well . . . " Shane said in a smooth tone of mock confidentiality, "since he holds the state record in the freestyle 50, 100, *and* 200—not to mention the *regional* records in the 100 and 200-metre butterfly *and* the 400-metre individual medley—I think the only thing he needs to worry about shaving is his legs."

"Not if Schroetter is swimming the 100-metre free for New Lennox in the nationals."

His smile flashed brilliantly, and his tone of voice was as cool and collected as one would expect from a confident and quick-witted guy like Rufus—a persona that he would do well to employ during his college interviews, I couldn't help thinking.

"Not a chance," he said, and for a moment he had me on the ropes . . . right up until his poised smile wavered—nothing more than a slight quiver at one corner of his mouth, but enough to let his classroom persona, Shane Guerin, peek through. But this was OK. I liked both Shane and Rufus and suspected that his true persona lived somewhere between the two anyway.

"No, I don't suppose there is," I conceded with a smile, tipping the scales back into his favor.

I sat at one of the pub tables along the wall opposite the counter, where I could see the intermittent traffic on the highway beyond the little strip mall's parking lot. While I ate, I could hear Shane and Kaitlin bickering and bartering good-naturedly over which cleanup tasks would be done by who. At one moment Kaitlin was begging, "Please, please, please, Shane, I really hate to mop, you know how much I hate it, so *pleeeeeeeeeeease . . .* " And Shane responded by telling her that he didn't know who this "Shane" guy was, but he sounded like a really cool guy, and he was sure if Kaitlin called him, this Shane guy would probably do the mopping for her. Then Kaitlin came back with, "All right, *Rufus*, would *you* do the mopping for me? Pretty *pretty* please?"

Of course, it couldn't be that easy—certainly not for Rufus. He wondered why there wasn't any sugar on top, prompting Kaitlin to refine her request to a "pretty pretty *pretty* please, with sugar on top?" to which Shane replied, "Just sugar? No cherries?" Kaitlin groaned and laughed at once as she whined an exasperated offer to clean the crisper, the desserts display, *and* the sinks, if only he—Rufus, not Shane, she was careful to add—would pretty *pretty* please, with sugar and cherries and whipped cream and sprinkles on top, do the mopping.

And the routine went on from there, with Kaitlin occasionally resorting to whining his name, and Shane whining hers right back, and both of them trying not to laugh.

By the time I'd finished eating, Shane had the greater half of the dining area mopped, but since he'd never actually responded in the affirmative to any of her pleas, Kaitlin could still be heard calling from the dessert display at the front of the shop, begging him to "please do the mopping, Rufus—I'm doing the dessert display right now, and it's got jelly and custard all over it, I swear—you'll really be getting the better end of the deal tonight!"

After he finished mopping the area in front of the pickup counter, he called out: "How do I know I can trust you? Did you *taste* the custard?"

With his fists wrapped around the top of the mop handle and his chin resting on his knuckles, Shane waited for the response, with mild relish. When it came ("Are you *kidding* me—*you* come taste it!"), he grinned and winked at me—a wink that said the best was yet to come.

"Well, just taste the jelly, at least," he called out. "Tell me if it's crusty or still moist."

"I *HATE* THAT WORD, AND YOU KNOW IT!"

"Which word?" he asked, still grinning. "Crusty?"

"MOIST!" she screech-groaned.

A moment passed. Shane waited patiently for the follow-up. And it came right on cue.

"Please, Rufus," Kaitlin pleaded through a tremor of exasperated laughter that made her voice sound hoarse, *"please* do the mopping for me!"

Shane gave me another wink before working his way toward the front of the shop with his mop. He'd mopped his way to the front counter and was looking at Kaitlin through the glass dessert display with a sly smile when I got up to use the bathroom. As I headed toward the back of the shop, I could hear him teasing sweetly, "All you had to do was ask. You know Rufus has got your back."

As I stood before the sink in the immaculate bathroom, washing my hands, I was still marvelling at the stark difference between the reserved kid I knew at school, and his confident alter ego at the bistro. And I couldn't help wondering if there was a little duality in all of us. Gordon had once said that everyone possesses multiple masks and that no one can ever know with any degree of certainty which mask represents the true nature of one's soul. He said that very few of us are ever truly capable of differentiating between our own masks, let alone the masks of others. He added that this was not a "conscious deception" but rather a "subconscious construct" or "mental firewall" to preserve sanity. He believed the masks we wear act as protective layers, that if one were to peel back those layers and discover the truth, the results would be irreparably devastating, and life as we know it would be unlivable.

Gordon told me this in the teachers' lounge during one of our Friday afternoon chats, shortly before his death. He looked at me with grave eyes through the bluish stream of smoke that trailed up from the tip of his hollow-point cigarette and said, "There *is* such a thing as too much knowledge, Jack." And then he smiled (though his eyes remained solemn) and said, "Just ask Mozart, or Proust, or Kurt Cobain. True knowledge comes with a price."

Gordon's words still echoed through my mind as I opened the bathroom door and stopped short. Directly across the narrow hall, the door to the storage room stood open (presumably to facilitate Shane's sweeping and mopping duties). But the open door isn't what stopped me in my tracks. It was the sight beyond the door. At the far end of the storage room, Shane was swapping his apron and work shirt for a T-shirt. He didn't see me because his back was to the doorway, and it was the sight of his back that caused me to halt. There were multiple bruises along the length of it, some faded, others which still looked a dark and angry shade of purple. As he pulled his T-shirt over his head, I stepped back and closed the bathroom door as quietly as possible.

I don't know how long I stood there holding the doorknob, but it must have been a while because when Shane passed by the door, he called out, "You didn't fall in there, did you, Mr. M.?"

I forced out a little laugh and told him I'd be right out. Then I flushed the toilet and washed my hands again.

The main lights were off, and the safety lights gleamed dimly as I made my way down the narrow hall and back into the dining area. Everything was spotless and ready for the morning crew. I looked around for Kaitlin, but she'd already headed off. Shane said that her boyfriend had picked her up, and that she said to say good-night for her and that she really enjoyed seeing me again.

Shane locked the door behind us, and while we stood on the little sidewalk in one of those awkward goodbye moments where nobody knows exactly what to say, I noticed that the parking lot was completely empty, save for my little blue Integra. I asked Shane if he needed a ride. He shook his head with a grateful smile and said that his dad would be picking him up. But there was something in his eyes, a telltale flicker, when he added, "He's usually late, he always forgets what time I get off, but he'll be here soon. I'll see you in class."

I nodded and went to my car, but as I fired up the engine, I caught sight of Shane in the rearview mirror. He was still watching me from the sidewalk, and the look in his eyes seemed a little too anxious. I backed out of the slot, but instead of driving off, I circled around and came to a stop in front of the bistro. Shane looked surprised when I rolled down the window, but he forced a nearly convincing smile as he raised a casual brow.

"I don't feel right about leaving you out here alone," I said. To the casual observer, it might have seemed a silly thing to say to a six-foot-tall nineteen-year-old athlete, but to me it didn't seem silly at all. He was one of my students, and I couldn't help but feel responsible. And I could see through his mask. I knew that no one was coming to pick him up. I knew that the moment my taillights vanished in the distance, he was going to head home on foot.

He tried again to convince me that he'd be all right, but I held firm. I told him that I could either wait with him until his dad showed up, or give him a ride. In the end, he opted for the ride and got in my car. But he left his alter ego Rufus at the bistro.

We pulled into Shane's driveway at 9:30 P.M.—which by my odometer would have been a twelve-mile walk for him. There was a dim light burning from what appeared to be the kitchen window. I turned off the headlights but left the engine running. Shane thanked me for the ride as he reached for the handle. I wanted to say something before he got out, something like "If you ever need to talk, I'm here," but I didn't want him to think that I knew something he didn't want anybody to know. I'd already caught him in the lie about his dad coming to pick him up, and I didn't want to cause him any further embarrassment, so I just told him to take it easy and that I'd see him in school. He thanked me again and got out of the car.

I was going to stay there until he got inside and then back out of the driveway before turning my headlights back on, but before Shane even got to the lawn, the porch light came on, and a man stepped outside and called out, "What have we got here?"

He was a tall man with broad shoulders, dressed in khaki shorts, a polo shirt, and sandals. He moved with a purpose down the porch steps and across the lawn at a brisk gait. Shane immediately put his head down and stood still as the man let out a sharp whistle and made a hand gesture toward my car.

"Hey," the man called out to me, "you want to kill that engine, son, and step out of the car?"

I did as he asked, without thinking. It was only when he got closer that I began to second guess my decision. He had a hard jaw line and piercing pale blue eyes that bored into you like a laser, and instinctively something inside me shifted, ready for a fight. But the guy didn't throw a punch or anything like that. He shot a glance at Shane and said, "I thought you said you were getting a ride from that girl you work with."

Shane said, "She didn't drive tonight. Her boyfriend dropped her off and picked her up. This is—"

The man looked at me and said, "Are you the boyfriend?"

Shane said, "No. This is Mr. McGregor. He's my teacher at school." He looked at me and said, "Mr. M., this is my dad."

The man's eyes narrowed, but he allowed a slight grin like maybe Shane was having him on. He made a sound that was almost a laugh, and his grin got a little wider, as if he'd just heard a joke that was almost funny. Then he made a precise beckoning gesture with the fingers of one hand and said, "Let's see some ID."

Shane said, "I'm not lying. He's really my teacher."

Shane's dad smiled at me and said, "Humor me."

I took out my wallet an held out the ID flap. When he asked me to take the ID out of the flap, Shane looked away in embarrassment. I took out the ID and handed it to Shane's dad. He scrutinized it with his piercing eyes before shooting a hard gaze at me.

"You don't look twenty-seven." He looked at the ID again and then back at me, as if searching for some telltale sign that would confirm his suspicion. Then he handed the ID back to me, and said, "You look like a kid. I'd card you for a six-pack. But that's just me." He thrust his hand forward, and his lips peeled back into a tight grin. "Doug Guerin."

"Jack McGregor," I said, accepting his handshake, which was one of those vice grip's intended to sting enough to elicit a flinch. It stung, but I didn't flinch. He must have appreciated my response because his grin broke into a fairly genuine-looking smile.

"Good to meet you, Jack," he said, and almost in the same breath, he added, "You're not an American. What're you, Irish?"

"Scottish."

"You're accent's a little muddled. How long have you been here?"

"Twelve years."

He nodded. "That would explain it. You try to sound like an American, and it muddles things up. Best to be true to your own heritage. You come over with your folks?"

I told him that I came over with my mother. I didn't mention my father or elaborate on why we'd left without him, and Shane's dad didn't press for any details. He simply nodded with an inscrutable expression then clapped his hands together (a sudden sound that gave Shane a jolt) and smiled like all was well. He shook my hand again and thanked me for getting his son home safely.

"Can't be too careful with kids running around at night, am I right, Jack?"

I wasn't sure if the question was rhetorical or if he expected an answer, so I just nodded. The small smile I managed to push out must have looked convincing enough because Doug Guerin nodded with approval and told his son that I was a good man and that he should pay attention because he could learn something from me.

Then he clapped his hands one more time and said, "Well, I really do appreciate your stepping up, Jack. Means a lot to me. But if you'll excuse us now, I've got some work to finish up, and I'm sure this one's got some homework that's due tomorrow. It was a real pleasure to meet you."

Shane offered a soft good-night and followed his dad into the house. I stood there in the driveway until the front door closed behind them, and the porch light went out. As I got back into my car and drove away, I felt an odd twinge of *déjà vu*, and couldn't shake off the feeling that I'd encountered Doug Guerin someplace before.

chapter six

back home/bad will hunting/one last dream

By the time I got back to my apartment, I was exhausted. It had been the longest day in recent memory, and all I wanted to do was fall onto my bed and drift off. But instead, I headed straight for the bathroom. I needed to take a shower, to wash away the day's events and clear the collision of dizzying thoughts from my head. It wasn't that easy, though. As I held my head under the pulsating wave, and the warm water sluiced down my back, the thoughts kept coming: the black matchbook I'd found in Gordon's drawer, my trip to The Black Otter, the surreal scene inside the Sigma, my pit stop at the little bistro on the way home, the sight of Shane Guerin's bruised back, the strange meeting with Shane's dad in the driveway, those piercing blue eyes boring into me, like the eyes of a Siberian Husky, curious yet calculating, probing for any signs of weakness.

Can't be too careful with kids running around at night, am I right, Jack?

Then suddenly an image from the past came flashing across my consciousness: my mother lifting up the back of my shirt in spite of my repeated protests that I was all right.

The sharp intake of her breath echoed back to me over the years, and in my mind's eye I could see myself looking over my shoulder at the reflection of my back in the mirror above the sink. I could see the angry bruises, and I knew that my mother knew the truth. I was fourteen at the time, and within less than a year, she'd saved and borrowed enough to get us out of the UK and as far away as possible, someplace he would never be able to find us.

I shook my head fast, trying to force the memory out of my mind. It vanished, but another memory rose to take its place. A more recent memory—one that would not go away . . .

Please, Mr. M., just let me crash here for tonight. I promise I won't be any trouble . . .

I came from the steamy bathroom a half hour later with a towel wrapped around my waist and went straight to the closet in my bedroom. My mind was still running with thoughts better left in the past, both recent and not so recent—thoughts that I was determined to eradicate, even if it meant diving in deeper.

I found the box of discs I was looking for on the top shelf of my bedroom closet. Not all of the discs inside were labeled, but the one I was looking for was. I took it to the DVD player in the living room. While the disc was loading, I unwrapped the pack of cigarettes I'd picked up on the way home and lit one before reclining on the sofa opposite the TV. My body was still dappled with moisture from the shower, and my wet hair hung in my eyes in a way that caused shutter-click memories of Abercrombie Boy from The Black Otter to flash at my periphery.

I let the disc run for a while without sound, just silent pictures from five years ago—a time when I'd felt infinitely more in control. I took a long hit off the cigarette while absently stroking my bare stomach with my free hand.

I watched the video, not really seeing it (the part I was looking for had yet to come up), seeing instead the images on the other side of the one-way glass back at The Black Otter . . . those stark images that had moved with slow, dreamlike precision, the touching and tasting and capering and cavorting, before the lights had gone out, and the curtain fell.

I exhaled a thin stream of smoke as I recalled the culmination of the ritual inside the Sigma.

I had closed my eyes because I didn't want to see. But somewhere along the way I must have opened them because, lying here now in the comfort and safety of my own living room, every detail came back to me with vivid clarity. Every touch, every caress, every whispered breath. In my mind I could see Ponytail's hand curling around the back of the boy's head and lifting it up as if it were as weightless as a balloon, their lips meeting, the tongue play between them. Then Ponytail hoisting the boy's legs and guiding himself in, followed by the nearly synchronized rocking of their hips. Ponytail with one hand on the boy's stomach, the other working the boy's erection as the boy's head tilted back as far as possible and his mouth fell open in a delirious cry of ecstasy.

I took another drag from the cigarette, and it burned going down my throat. I crushed it out in the ashtray on the coffee table, with a grimace.

He had been waiting for me in the circular drive outside The Black Otter. Ponytail.

He was leaning against my car, casually smoking a cigarette, when I came out. His red hair hung down to his shoulders, straight and shiny, giving his angular face a softer, gentler appearance. I tried not to look at him as I came down the steps. I half pretended to be looking for the valet, who was nowhere in sight. Before I got to the bottom of the steps, Ponytail held up a hand and smiled at me. Wrapped around the third finger of his right hand was my key ring.

He jingled the keys with a sly look and then tossed them to me as he flicked his cigarette away. He was still smiling when he stood up straight and reached into the breast pocket of his expensive suit jacket, but his smile held none of the animal malice it had when he'd stared me down from the opposite side of the observation window.

He drew a card from his wallet and held it out between his index and middle fingers. I took the card without reading what was printed on it. His eyes were still on me, and it was hard to look away from them. He smiled more openly and tongued his crooked canine absently.

"Matt Grayson," he said, without offering his hand, but there was no guile in his pale blue eyes. "Call me sometime, if you'd like to get together. That's my cell number at the bottom. Any time, night or day."

And without another word, he strode to the red Testarossa that was parked in front of my car, fired up the engine, and sped off.

Images passed by on the TV screen like archive footage in a studio screening room: high school kids performing scenes in my drama class five years ago. And still, all I could see were the taillights of that shiny red Ferrari winking in the darkness of the night as Matt Grayson, aka Ponytail, disappeared from view.

When the taillights in my mind faded, the image of the boy on the bench returned, melding with the painting that leaned against the wall across the room.

On the TV screen, a clapboard was featured with "GOOD WILL HUNTING" printed in the title block. A rolling flutter followed, then my former students Mickey Greenleaf and Marilyn Plath were featured in bed. I didn't turn up the volume, I didn't need to. I could've quoted the scene verbatim. In a minute Mickey would jump out of the bed, clad only in his boxers, and begin the painful outpouring of emotion that would culminate with him/Will telling Marilyn/Skylar that he didn't love her. It had been Mickey's idea that the students be allowed to perform scenes from movies instead of plays for their finals. At the time, I'd thought it a harmless request, but now I wasn't so certain. Now it felt like, in giving Mickey his way, I had handed him a weapon to publicly humiliate and crush his rival with.

You know that they were rivals over you . . . we used to call it The Mickey and Marilyn Smackdown . . . they would actually fight over you!

Keeping my eyes on the screen, I used the remote control to bring up my music library on the computer across the room. I didn't have the Aerosmith version of *Come Together,* but I did have the original version by The Beatles, and as the music came from the speakers, Mickey stood up in his boxers and started shouting at Marilyn, who knelt on the bed in her silk robe, looking genuinely wounded.

His physical resemblance to the actor whose role he was playing aside, Mickey appeared to be giving a performance that relied less on mimicry and more on instinct. His body language accentuated the complex emotions of the character so effectively that even with the sound off, the inner turmoil came through. He spoke with his eyes in a way that few actors can without tipping their hand, and when he pulled back from Marilyn's touch in the big moment, his self-loathing was so cannily on the mark that I would have looked away had not his very presence on screen commanded my attention with such unyielding magnetism. When he told Marilyn that he didn't love her, the blade dug as deeply into his own heart as it did into hers—but watching this little video clip now, I could see something that I hadn't noticed before: the unequivocal cruelty in his eyes as the final blow is delivered and Marilyn is left devastated and alone.

When this disc was played for my drama class on that cool spring afternoon five years ago, there followed a silence unlike any I had witnessed before or since—students whose final projects had yet to be screened were understandably overwhelmed; those who had already had their shot at bat were equally impressed. In the ensuing applause, I noticed that while Mickey was beaming as if he'd just won the

Academy Award, Marilyn could manage little more than a humble smile . . . one that scarcely touched her glassy eyes.

A month later at Awards Night, Mickey and Marilyn were together again (so far as I know or can tell, for the last time), smiling for the Canaima Reader's sole photographer after being named Best Actor and Best Actress of the year. The scene was a virtual repeat of their crowning moment in my class after their *Good Will Hunting* video was screened: Mickey beaming at the approbation of his peers, Marilyn bravely affecting a gracious smile.

After the ceremony, I found her sitting on the steps in the hall outside of the gym, her trophy (a fairly decent knockoff of the Tony Award) looking lonesome three steps below her. Like everyone else in my class, she knew that I had agreed to sponsor Mickey at Canaima Community College's summer stock theater program, and she knew that would mean the two of us, Mickey and I, would be spending a good deal of the summer together.

She also knew that, in my class, Mickey was "teacher's pet."

It was no secret really—everyone knew it. Mickey was a talented actor, and I was a dedicated drama teacher. He was the prize pupil that every teacher dreams of, the one that you can guide to a remarkable career, the one that will eventually thank you for that guidance at an awards ceremony that's being broadcast to the entire world.

Marilyn didn't look at me when I sat next to her on the steps. She accepted my congratulations much the same way she'd accepted the award itself, with a gracious smile and sad eyes. We spoke of summer plans, and she told me that she would be taking a few courses at Drake before heading off to CMU in the fall. I asked a few polite questions about the classes she'd be taking at Drake, whether they'd be drama related or not, carefully skirting the Mickey issue and my own summer plans. She said she would be taking a few prerequisite theater courses as well as a calculus course that she wanted to get out of the way. She would also be auditioning for the children's one acts in July. I told her that I would be glad to write a letter of recommendation, and I meant it. She was a very promising actress, and I would have done anything to help her reach her full potential. She smiled in a way that made me feel guiltier than I would have thought possible.

It wasn't until I rose to leave that she let something slip—something she had debated telling me for some time, perhaps even as far back as spring break when she'd first started working with Mickey on their *Good Will Hunting* scene for my class.

Her words came out softly but decisively: "You don't know him, Mr. McGregor."

She didn't look at me when she said this; her gaze was locked on the little award three steps down from her, but the statement had more than enough impact without the added pressure of her heartbreaking gaze on me.

At the time it had felt like an accusation, perhaps even a veiled threat—one that could have led to all sorts of discomfort for me and possibly threatened my job security. I was a twenty-two-year-old high school teacher who had played favorites with an extremely attractive male student—an eighteen-year-old student, but still a student—and everyone knew it. That same student had dropped by my apartment on more than a few occasions during the fall and spring semesters. Uninvited of course, but that wouldn't have mattered to the school board, nor to concerned parents. He'd even crashed on my couch a few of those times—once on a school night, and several students had seen him getting out of my car in the faculty parking lot the following morning.

It had been a dangerous time, even if I hadn't fully realized it until my chat with Marilyn Plath on the steps outside of the main gym on Awards Night. The slightest breath of an inappropriate relationship between myself and Mickey Greenleaf could have spelled my professional demise in no uncertain terms. Not that there was anything inappropriate about my relationship with Mickey. In fact, I would have been able to swear on my word that he had received no special consideration from me, at least none that hadn't been warranted by his performance in class or on the stage. On the other hand, I would have been hard-pressed to swear that I had no other interest in the boy beyond the academic or extracurricular activities related to my job as his teacher.

You don't know him, Mr. McGregor.

But it hadn't been an accusation. And it hadn't been a threat, either. I understood this now. It had been a warning, the kind you would expect from a trusted friend or family member whose sole concern is your well being and safety. The tone of Marilyn's voice had been soft, but the warning was clear: *Don't let him suck you in, Mr. McGregor. Get away from him while you still can. He's gonna break your heart the same way he did mine.*

Or had she been driving at something else altogether? Had there been something deeper, perhaps even darker, about Mickey Greenleaf that even his biggest fan, and most devoted teacher, had yet to see?

This I didn't know. Not yet. Not for sure, anyway.

I *did* know that the answers to my questions weren't going to be found by watching a five-year-old video recording of a class project while listening to the randomly selected background music of a kinky patron at The Black Otter.

I reached for the remote and stopped the video, which by now was more than halfway through the following class project—a fairly authentic and reasonably gory recreation of the final showdown in *Reservoir Dogs*, with a skinny sixteen-year-old named Mason Elliot giving a particularly grueling rendition of Tim Roth's Mr. Orange bleeding to death while holding the other zoot-suited dogs at bay with his 9mm BB pistol.

I sat back in my towel, my hair still damp but slowly

drying, and again the image of the ponytailed redhead leaning against my car outside of The Black Otter resurfaced. The image of him flicking his cigarette away and holding up his right hand and jingling my key ring. And yet his playful smile appeared to be at cross purposes with his gaze.

But still, he had been close to the boy in the Sigma room, close enough to know, *really* know...*if* he'd known what to look for, which, of course, he hadn't.

He'd never met the real Mickey Greenleaf.

He'd never opened the door to his apartment to find Mickey inside watching the Cartoon Network while drinking a glass of milk; he'd never seen Mickey look up at him with those bright and innocent eyes.

I'm sorry about this, Mr. M. I just needed a place to unwind—my dad's on the warpath again, and my mom's cheering him on. Could I crash here tonight? Just tonight. Things'll be better tomorrow, and I'll go home, I promise.

It had only been a handful of nights that he'd crashed at my apartment—two weeks worth of nights at the most, I'm positive. He'd kept some of his things there—a toothbrush, a few T-shirts, a pair of jeans, a couple of CDs—a handful of incidentals, things that he would easily be able to collect and throw into his book bag if he needed them. Every now and then he would borrow a pair of my shorts after a shower while his things were in the wash. Other times he would just watch TV on the couch with the towel around his waist. And always he slept on the couch in his boxers with the spare comforter from the hall closet wrapped around him.

On occasion, I would wake from restless sleep and find my way into the living room, and there would be Mickey, the comforter kicked down by his feet, or in a heap off the side of the couch. Before returning to bed, I would always pull the comforter back up to his shoulders and make sure that it was tucked in at the back of the couch just in case he got restless in his sleep again.

Maybe once or twice I'd sat on the chair to the side of the couch, or on the edge of the coffee table in front of it, and watched him sleep—just to make sure there were no bad dreams—and while listening to the sound of his breathing, I might have reached out to stroke his hair when he stirred. Sometimes I left the hall light on low, in case he woke, and, forgetting where he was, became frightened or disoriented. Always, I would leave my door at the end of the hall open in case he needed anything.

Please, Mr. M., just let me crash here for tonight, I swear it'll be the last time.

It never seemed to be the last time, though—not until the end of the summer following his graduation when he disappeared. He was supposed to have gone off to college in LA, but no one ever heard from him after he'd left home that fall. Speculation and rumors had circulated among the drama kids at school for a while, but, as with all things out of sight, in time the collective interest in what had become of West High's Golden boy began to fade. Though it took longer for me than most, eventually Mickey Greenleaf began to recede into that depthless place within, where memories go to rest until something, or someone, comes along to stir them from their slumber.

I stared at the pack of cigarettes on the coffee table. Though I hadn't even been able to finish the first, I suddenly wanted another, as if the poison within could be vanquished by an external dose. I wanted to smoke it the way Matt Grayson had done while leaning against my car outside of The Black Otter. I wanted to look tough and cool and in total control, like him.

But as I lay back on the couch, my eyes became heavy, and my desire for the poison couldn't overcome the fact that I was running on empty and ready to crash.

As my eyelids drooped, the image of Marilyn Plath resurfaced in my mind—not on the steps outside of the gym, though. It was the image of her in bed with Mickey before the part where he leaps up and explodes on her. She had looked so naive, her heart so nakedly exposed, as she stroked Mickey's bare back and spoke of her life plans. I had known that she wasn't just acting. She was speaking dialogue that had been written for an actress, but there was something beneath that dialogue that was real and true. Something that extended beyond the script, a very real emotion that had made the scene all the more believable.

Mickey lay silent with his head in her lap, his eyes closed in unconscious imitation of himself on my couch.

Then in my mind, Marilyn looked up from the scene and, not entirely out of character, said: *You don't know him, Mr. McGregor,* while she continued to caress Mickey's bare back in long, gentle strokes. Then as she went back into her soundless delivery of the scripted word, Mickey opened his eyes and without moving a muscle projected this: *Don't believe her, Mr. M. She doesn't know me the way you do.*

A single tear streamed down his cheek. And suddenly his watery blue eyes were covered with an oversized blindfold, and the hand stroking his back was longer and stronger, with nails that had been clipped blunt. A facile hand, elegant yet distinctly masculine. It stopped in mid-stroke at Mickey's shoulder, and then crept around to Mickey's mouth, where the forefinger slid in between those sweetly parted lips.

Sitting on the bed now, with Mickey's head in his lap, was Matt Grayson. They were both naked and hungry. And in a gentle flash, they were no longer on the bed in the video but on the couch in my living room.

I watched them from my place on the coffee table, while in the recliner off to the side sat Gordon Powell. There was a canvas on the easel before him, a fine brush in one hand and a lighter in the other; clamped between his teeth was a freshly lit hollow-point cigarette. He snapped the lighter shut and took a deep drag as he applied gentle brushstrokes to the canvas.

But he wasn't painting Mickey Greenleaf or Matt Grayson. He wasn't even facing them.

He was painting me.

And just like that I was no longer sitting on the edge of the coffee table but bound to the bench in the Sigma room, like the boy in Gordon's painting. I was blindfolded but somehow I could see Matt Grayson smiling at me as he continued to drive his forefinger in slow thrusts, deeper and deeper into Mickey's mouth, while Gordon added more gentle brushstrokes to his canvas and hummed Pearl Jam's *Nothing as it Seems* softly under his breath.

Then Mickey looked at me with heartbreaking sincerity as he continued to suck Matt Grayson's forefinger in long, deliberate thrusts.

See? He likes it, Ponytail said, but Mickey's eyes said differently. They called to me in a way that made my own eyes burn with hot tears beneath the blindfold.

I began to struggle with the straps that pinned my wrists to the board above my head. But my naked body only moved in a dreamy sort of slow motion, and Ponytail Grayson said: *Now you know what he feels—is it everything you expected?*

But I wasn't listening to him. I was struggling even harder to free myself, and Ponytail was laughing at me, which made me struggle all the more until Gordon stopped humming and spoke without looking up from his canvas: *Stop wriggling about and lie still, Jack, you'll spoil the fresco!*

Gordon, please— I cried without parting my lips. But Gordon only made a soothing shushing sound as he continued to work on his painting.

Mickey's eyes were still on me. A runner of drool spilled from the corner of his lips and lathered Ponytail's forefinger. Ponytail smiled as he continued driving his finger into Mickey's mouth.

The girl was right, Jack! Gordon whispered, conspiratorially. *The boy is an apple-polisher! I told you so! Don't let him work his magic on you! Give him an inch, and you'll fall under his spell as swift as a swallow and slick as a fingerfucker! Use your eyes, man! Nothing's as it seems! Now open your fucking eyes and see!*

I opened my eyes for a split second and saw Doug Guerin, Shane's dad, standing at the far side of the viewing room where I lay bound to the bench. He was blocking the secret doorway, beyond which a shadowy figure knelt. In Doug Guerin's clenched fist there was a leather belt, the loose end of which dangled at his side. His icy blue gaze bored into me as the shiny buckle at the end of the belt gleamed in the dim light.

And then, just as quickly as the image had come, it was gone, as if it had never been at all. And in the complete darkness that followed, all I could see were the three who had been there with me all along—all of them as they were before: Mickey drooling, Ponytail laughing, Gordon humming and painting.

I woke with a jolt, but I didn't cry out.

I was alone in my apartment, lying on the couch with the towel still wrapped around my waist. My hair was dry. I pushed it back from my eyes and let out a short, staggered sigh that sounded more like a shudder.

As I shook off the last remnants of the dream, I looked around and immediately my sight fell on the image of the canvas across the room. The naked boy that Gordon had painted—and not through the one-way glass of the viewing room but from *inside* the Sigma. By the angle of his frame, it was obvious that Gordon had been up close when he'd painted the boy in bondage.

As I wiped the sleep from my eyes, I didn't have to wonder if Gordon had paid full price for the privilege of painting his subject in privacy. The real question was: Had the boy on the bench known that he was being committed to canvas? And if so, had he known just who he was sitting for?

For the moment, I could only guess at the answer. If I wanted to know the truth, I would have to go back to the mansion on the hill.

And this time I would have to get *inside* the Sigma—close enough to remove that oversized blindfold and look my former student in the eye.

chapter seven

the greeting card/the other painting/ the eyes of the white wolf

I WOKE LATE THE FOLLOWING MORNING, FEELING A LITTLE HUNG over and wondering if the previous night's events had just been part of a dream, or possibly an hallucination brought on by something that might have been slipped into the *hors d'oeuvres* I'd consumed in The Black Otter's lounge. I was still floating in a cloud of confusion when I discovered a cream-coloured envelope that had been slid under the door of my apartment while I was sleeping. There was no stamp on it and no return address. My name was handwritten in neat block letters, which were centered on the envelope's face. The back flap was sealed by a circle of maroon wax with the initials MKG stamped into it.

Two names came to mind instantly as I stared at those initials. One I had known for the better part of the last decade; the other I had heard for the first time just last night.

I opened the envelope with a kitchen knife and pulled out the greeting card inside. It was the same creamy shade as the envelope, but its cover was bordered in a regal blue and featured an image: a naked young man sitting on a small island rock in the middle of a Greek channel, with his arms wrapped around his knees, which were drawn up close to his chest. The image of this young man brought to mind another image: Rodin's Thinker, with his chiseled frame and thoughtful countenance, frozen in timeless contemplation. Only the face of the young man in this painting seemed more forlorn than thoughtful.

There was a message of sorts handwritten on the inside:

The night has a thousand eyes,
And the day but one;
Yet the light of the bright world dies
With the dying sun.

The mind has a thousand eyes,
And the heart but one;
Yet the light of a whole life dies
When love is done.

It was a poem by Bourdillon, one that I'd last seen almost five years ago. Written on a sheet of notebook paper that had been left on my kitchen counter the morning after Mickey's last sleepover. Centered on top of the note was a shiny red apple. The message below the poem read:

Dear Mr. M,
Thanks for believing in me, and for trying to make me a better person. I hope I don't disappoint you too much. I'll see you at Christmas break, if you'll have me. I'll be nineteen by then, but I promise to stay on the couch unless you say otherwise. I'm really sorry about last night. I was just messed up because of the fight with my dad. Nobody has ever cared about me the way you do, and I just wanted you to know that I appreciate everything you've done for me. I'm going to make you proud.

Wait and see, things will be different when I come back.

Mickey

But he hadn't come back. Not at Christmas break and not the following summer. The sheet of notebook paper beneath the apple was the last I'd ever heard from him.

I'd read that note countless times, and relived the last night I'd seen him over and over again. Even now I can see it as if it were yesterday.

Mr. M . . . Jack . . . are you awake?

I'd heard him calling to me in a soft whisper from the doorway, but I remained on my side with my head against the pillow and my eyes closed.

Then he was closer, whispering something about being cold, even though it was a mild late summer night. And then I could feel the blankets shifting and the bed sinking a little as he climbed in and moved close to me. He'd taken off his shirt before coming into the room; I could feel his bare chest against my back, the swell beneath his boxers pressing against me. For some reason, I continued to pretend to be asleep, even when he put his hand on my shoulder and gently pulled me onto my back . . .

Lines from that final message came flooding into my consciousness in a rapid flow now.

Thanks for believing in me . . . I hope I don't disappoint you . . . I'm really sorry . . . Nobody has ever cared about me . . . I'm going to make you proud . . . things will be different when I come back.

I looked at the greeting card. The poem was the same, but there was no personal message below it this time. There was only a symbol—one that I recognized all too well:

$$\Sigma$$

Below the symbol, there was a flat brass key affixed to the card by a single strip of clear tape. The key bore a four-digit number, and the warning: DO NOT REPRODUCE.

I turned the card over, but there was no message on the back, either. I peeled the key from the card, careful to preserve the strip of tape, but there wasn't even so much as a thumbprint embedded on its sticky side.

I studied the poem and tried to recall Mickey's handwriting—as many times as I'd read his final note (not to mention all the papers he'd written for my class), I couldn't be certain either way. The neat little block letters could have been printed by anyone.

It wasn't difficult to imagine Mickey doing something mysterious like slipping a card with a coded message and key under my door—his flair for the dramatic had been fairly limitless back in the day. But for him to send me a message not only after all these years of silence but on the very day after my visit to The Black Otter—where I'd just happened to view an erotic performance artist who bore a striking resemblance to him—that would have been a pretty far-fetched coincidence.

The initials stamped into the wax seal on the envelope certainly fit like a puzzle piece: Michael Kevin Greenleaf. But those same initials could also stand for Matthew Kyle Grayson, aka Ponytail.

A voice that sounded like the ghost of the late Gordon Powell chimed inside my head: *Another apple-polisher. Don't let them suck you into their little game, Jack. Fuck 'em.*

The sudden warning duly noted, my thoughts drifted back to the night before—after the scene inside the Sigma had played out. I could see myself standing at the top of the stone steps outside The Black Otter while in the circular drive below Matt Grayson leaned against my car with his knowing smile and cool blue eyes as he jingled my keys.

Call me sometime if you'd like to get together. That's my cell number at the bottom. Anytime, night or day.

The look in his eye had been very different from the challenging leer he'd projected from his side of the one-way glass—so different, in fact, that had I not just witnessed his "performance" inside the Sigma, I would have been completely clueless to the darker nature that resided behind the friendly mask.

The notion that the card with the key had come from Matt Grayson and not Mickey grew stronger the more I thought about it. But the poem written on the inside still needled at me. Only Mickey would have known about the poem, so if Matt Grayson was the one who'd sent the card, it would stand to reason that he'd heard about the poem from Mickey. And if that was the case, it would also stand to reason that my assumption was correct: the boy strapped to the bench inside the Sigma had indeed been Mickey Greenleaf.

But why send me the card? Why include the poem? And what was the key for?

It all seemed like a puzzle conveniently falling into place. A neat and tidy little capper to a chance encounter that stemmed from a purely random series of discoveries: the painting of the boy in bondage, the matchbook (with its own coded message) in the drawer of Gordon's night table, the secluded mansion buried in the wooded hills up north—

Unless . . .

I went to my room and found the matchbook where I'd left it, inside the wooden box on my dresser. I opened the flap and held the matchbook side by side with the greeting card. Though the messages on each were written in different languages, both looked similar enough that they could have been written by the same hand.

A tiny wave of tendrils ascended my spine as I thought back to the day I'd discovered the painting of the boy in bondage in Gordon's apartment. In my mind, I could see it leaning against the wall, amidst the clutter of several other canvases. But there had been something different about it, something that set it apart from the others. I closed my eyes and concentrated on the memory of that discovery.

It came to me in a sudden and lucid flash. While the top edges of the other paintings against the wall had all been caked in a layer of dust, the fresco of the boy in bondage had looked pristine, as if it had recently been dusted . . . or recently *placed* there.

The same had been true with the matchbook, which had been in perfect condition when I'd found it on top of all the other dusty odds and ends in the drawer of the bedside table. Like the painting, it was as if it had been deliberately placed there *after* Gordon's death.

At the back of my mind, I could hear the warning Marilyn Plath had given me on the steps outside of the main gym on Senior Awards Night five years earlier.

You don't know him, Mr. McGregor.

She had been speaking of Mickey, of course. But right now, I wasn't thinking about Mickey, because there was something else tugging at the periphery of my thoughts. Something I had missed. Forgotten. Something vital.

I took a deep calming breath, and it came.

I headed back into the living room, to the front closet, where I'd stored the packing crate which contained the painting that Gordon's older brother, Arthur C. Powell, had sent back to me—the *other* painting Gordon had done under the pseudonym of Ivan Duprez. It had arrived early on a Tuesday, just as I was heading out the door for school, so I'd simply placed the crate inside the front closet, without bothering to open it. And with all the discoveries that had followed, I'd completely forgotten about the sealed painting in the closet. Until now.

I set the crate against the wall in the foyer and wrenched it open with the claw end of a hammer. The fastening nails squealed in mild protest, but the cover came off with relative ease. I set it aside and immediately began to peel away the protective layers of shredded packing material.

I halted abruptly when the surface of the canvas was revealed. Nearly identical to the image on the cover of the greeting card, the painting was of a naked young man with his arms wrapped around his bent legs, which were pulled up close to his chest. Though his face was obscured by the long hair, which spilled down to his shoulders, I recognized him at once. He was Matt Grayson, aka Ponytail from The Black Otter. I could see it not only in the shape of his long, chiseled body and auburn hair, both perfectly replicated by Gordon's brush, but also in the pale blue eyes that gazed with cool intent from the shadowy veil of those bangs.

As I stared at the painting, a frightening question rose at the back of my mind and sent a fresh wave of chilly tendrils racing over my body: If the boy bound to the bench in the Sigma room at The Black Otter was indeed Mickey, had he been there of his own volition, or had he been forced to be there?

No one had heard from him since he'd taken off at the end of that summer five years ago. Was it possible that he'd fallen in with the wrong crowd and spent the past five years in captivity? Or that he'd been brainwashed by a cult and become a mindless drone? Certainly the staff at The Black Otter, with their peculiar affectation of deportment and cool detachment, could qualify as members of a cult. And certainly Mickey, with his rough home life and propensity for drama, was the type who could easily be wooed by the opulence and intrigue of the environment, as well as its smooth-talking, well-groomed occupants—a fraternity of physical perfection where he would fit right in.

Mickey had often been drawn to danger. Not willfully, or even consciously, like some boys. But if risk was in his orbit, more likely than not, Mickey would find himself sucked into its gravitational pull. Of course, this is not to say that he was entirely innocent—rarely, if ever, had Mickey put up any resistance to danger. I'm only saying that, to the best of my knowledge, he did not actively seek out dangerous situations. Contrary to what I'm sure Gordon Powell would have thought, I don't believe that Mickey's visits to my apartment—or the occasional sleepovers—had anything to do with a conscious desire to flirt with danger. Or at least I hadn't believed it at the time.

Back then I'd believed that he was just a troubled kid in need of a safe place. A place where he could lower his guard, step down from the stage, and just be himself. And he had done precisely that. He had trusted me enough to drop the façade and tell me things that he could never tell his friends at school.

He'd sat on my couch and told me all about his turbulent relationship with his father. He'd admitted that his mother had spoiled him, and allowed that this was likely the primary cause for his father's antagonism toward him. But the events he'd described weren't of the sort that arise from the average father-son clashes. They were acts of violence and abuse, the likes of which I was all too familiar with from my own upbringing.

With one notable difference.

While my father had been an aggressive drunk, who'd had no compunction about leaving a lasting mark (on occasion, he would proudly order me to lift my shirt to show his drinking mates the "what for" he'd given me), Mickey's old man employed more "sophisticated" methods of punishment.

He does these things to me, Mr. M.—things that he used to do when he was in Afghanistan.

Mickey's father had done three tours in the Middle East and had learned countless techniques that left little to no physical evidence of abuse. Mickey had described in chilling detail what it was like to be forced to stand naked in the shower with the cold water running on him from above while periodic power blasts came straight at his face, body, and groin from the garden hose his father had fed through the bathroom window—a punishment that could last anywhere from twenty minutes to an hour, depending on the infraction.

Other punishments included a rubber band repeatedly snapped on the top of his head, where his hair would conceal the welts; kneeling on the concrete basement floor with his head tilted as far back as it would go and his arms outstretched while holding two of his father's dumbbells perfectly parallel to his shoulders (this would be done in ten minute stretches, with thirty-second breaks, and could last upwards of two hours); being forced to eat a can of dog food (this particular "corrective action" had occurred on Mickey's thirteenth birthday when he'd failed to clean his dinner plate but still had room for a slice of cake).

But one incident stood above and well beyond all others, crossing the line from unimaginable abuse to irrefutable torture. According to Mickey, it had happened shortly after he'd spent the night at my place and been seen getting out of my car in the faculty parking lot the following morning. Somehow his father had gotten wind of the story, and when Mickey came home from school a few days later, his father took him down to the basement. He instructed Mickey to lie down on the bench press with his arms at his sides, then he wrapped a bed sheet around Mickey's upper body, pinning him to the bench (his father never used a rope to secure him, because rope left marks). Mickey said it was the most frightening thing his father had ever done to him because while it was happening his father's eyes didn't look human.

They looked like the eyes of those wolves. You know, those white wolves with those really intense blue eyes? His eyes looked like that, I swear it, Mr. M.

Before the horror show began, Mickey's father calmly explained what he was about to do. He said it was a technique he'd used in Iraq to extract information from the enemy. He told his son that there was nothing to worry about, that he would not be in any life-threatening danger, but assured him that after the "interrogation" was completed Mickey would tell him anything he wanted to know.

Mickey had never resisted any of his father's other punishments, figuring that if he remained silent and took it like a man it would be over more quickly, and that if he resisted or pleaded it would only last longer.

But this time he did resist. This time he pleaded with his father to tell him what it was that he'd done wrong. He swore that he would confess to anything. His father smiled a sad smile and told Mickey it didn't work that way. He said he knew that Mickey was scared, that he could hear his heart pounding, and assured him that this was a normal reaction. He told Mickey that the fear he was feeling was a good thing, a "cleansing" thing, and assured him that he himself would take no pleasure in seeing his son suffer, but it had to be this way.

Mickey trembled as he recounted what happened next, and I had to resist the urge to place a comforting hand on his shoulder, for fear that he would break down and not be able to continue.

His father knelt beside the bench and kissed him on the forehead. Then he placed a towel over the boy's face and slowly poured water over the towel. When Mickey began to choke and convulse, his father would remove the towel and lift his son's head up for a breather. Then he would replace the towel for another go.

Mickey wasn't sure how many times the procedure was repeated, but after the second time under the flow, he begged his father to let him confess to whatever it was that he'd done. This was before he'd begun to lose all rational thought and the fear of drowning had become his sole focus.

His father never did ask him any questions. Only after it was over and Mickey lay on the bench, coughing so hard that his lungs burned, did his father finally speak. He told Mickey that he had eyes everywhere, that there was nothing

Mickey could do, say, or think that wouldn't get back to him. He said that he was a soldier and that his son was a soldier too, whether he knew it or not. He told Mickey to come see him if he ever started to have feelings that were less than manly. He told him that his old man had the cure and that Mickey would be bent back into the correct posture, or broken and reset like a bone, if necessary.

His parting warning had come more directly to the point: "Next time you need a ride to school after you've been out all night, you call me. Or you walk. I will not be publicly humiliated by your antics. Don't let me hear that you've been with that boy again."

I hadn't thought that last statement odd at the time, but thinking back on it now, something *did* feel odd. It wasn't that his father had believed that Mickey had spent the night with a fellow classmate—I was only twenty-two back then, and early on, even a few hall monitors had mistaken me for a student. It was the uncomfortable shift in Mickey's expression when he'd repeated his father's final warning. As if he'd gone one too far and spilled a telling piece of information.

Don't let me hear that you've been with that boy again.

Only now it didn't make sense. If someone who'd seen Mickey getting out of my car in the faculty parking lot that morning had relayed the story to Mickey's father, wouldn't that same someone have told him that I was a teacher?

Of course, it was possible that the witness who'd seen us getting out of my car had been a family friend who'd simply assumed that I was a schoolmate. But from the portrait that Mickey had painted of his father—a cunning and precise ex-military man, who crossed every T and dotted every I—it was difficult to believe that a guy like that wouldn't have conducted a thorough investigation and found out exactly who I was.

Either way, I was now convinced that I was *not* "that boy" Mickey's old man had warned him to stay away from.

But still, this was merely another piece on the fringes of

the ever-growing puzzle. I needed to fill in all those missing center pieces, and there was only one place I could do that.

I looked at the greeting card, then shifted my gaze to the two paintings across the room, one still in its crate, the other propped against the wall, and said softly, "All right, we'll play it your way."

I wasn't sure just which of the two paintings this little surge of bravado was intended for, but I was determined to find out.

chapter eight

return to the black otter/pseudonyms/ the other side of the looking-glass

I LEFT MY APARTMENT AT QUARTER AFTER 6:00 P.M. AND ARRIVED at The Black Otter shortly before 8:00. I'd stopped off along the way to get some cash so I wouldn't have to use my credit card to pay for a private sitting in the Sigma. This was probably a hollow gesture, considering that whoever had slipped the greeting card under my door already knew my name and address, but still, I felt it would be prudent not to leave a paper trail. Despite its elegant façade and impeccable staff, The Black Otter was an establishment where patrons paid to have sex with young men, and even though I had no intention of committing an illegal act, I was pretty sure that a receipt billed to my credit card for a private room in a house of prostitution would be considered fairly damning evidence—more than enough to cost me my job and make it next to impossible for me to secure employment at any high school in the country.

I pulled into the wide curve at the end of the drive and came to a stop. As before, the valet appeared out of nowhere. He wasn't the kid from the previous night, but both his manner of dress and appearance were the same:

black trousers, crisp white tunic, flawless complexion, dazzling smile. With his blond hair slicked back and shaved at the sides, he looked as if he'd just stepped from the pages of an F. Scott Fitzgerald novel.

He handed me a glossy black card, and I gave him my spare key. I watched him drive around the side of the mansion, taking note of the direction he'd headed, in case the need for a hasty departure arose. Then I headed up the steps to the front door.

I was greeted by the broad-shouldered doorman with the dark hair and darker eyes. He didn't take me to the little dressing room down the short hallway (I'd had the foresight to come in a jacket and tie this time), and he didn't take me to the lounge for refreshments either. Instead, he led the way straight to the front desk and informed me that Devon would be around "in a jiffy." It seemed an odd expression, coming from a young guy. But then everything at The Black Otter seemed odd in one way or another.

Shortly after the doorman had gone, I noticed a leather-bound ledger sitting on the desk. Close enough that I could reach it and flip through the pages without drawing attention—just a quick little peek to see if there might be any clue in those pages that might help me . . . perhaps the name of a certain employee who *didn't* work as a valet or a greeter or a desk clerk. Perhaps the ledger contained the names of both the patron and the young man I'd seen in the Sigma the night before. If so, and if the name of that young man happened to be Michael Greenleaf, then I would at least know that Mickey was not being held here against his will, that he was merely an employee, like the doorman or Devon the desk clerk. Of course, I would need to see him in person, either way—there were far too many questions that needed answering, and I felt sure that Mickey would be able to shed more than a little light on many of them—but to know in advance that he was here of his own free will would certainly ease my tension.

My hand moved, but before it even got close to the ledger, a voice called out: "Ah ah ah, no peeking."

It came in a friendly teasing manner, but my cheeks burned with guilt as I turned to face the smiling man who stood in the wide archway between the lounge and the lobby. He was a tall man in his late-fifties, tanned and handsome, with a full head of black hair that was just beginning to grey at the temples. His dark eyes were a bit intense but friendly. His big smile was showy but genuine, like the smile of a movie star in a comfortable setting off camera. He wasn't a movie star, but he was famous. I'd seen him on cable news programs, where his smile looked just as showy but nowhere near as genuine. He approached and placed a hand on my shoulder.

"I'm just messing with you," he said, giving my shoulder a fatherly squeeze. Then, with a wink, he added, "I won't tell if you won't tell."

He opened the ledger and riffled through the pages. I watched as the lines of entries floated by. He stopped at one page and tapped his finger on an entry for the Gamma room dated one week ago. Then he slid his finger down to the name listed below: MR. DORIAN GRAY.

"That's me," he said, with a conspiratorial wink and grin. "They're committed to confidentiality here. Very hush-hush. Everyone has a code name. When was your last visit?"

The blunt question took me by surprise, and I froze. Mr. "Dorian Gray" chuckled amicably at my blush and said, "Don't tell me. Let me see if I can get it on my own."

He turned the pages in rapid succession, scanning each with the alacrity of a man who is used to reading copious amounts of paperwork in the pursuit of a single minute detail. He stopped when he reached the entries from the night before, and his finger landed decisively on the entry for the Sigma at 7:45 P.M. The name listed directly below was: MR. JEAN-PAUL VALLEY. Like Dorian Gray, the pseudonym "Jean-Paul Valley" was borrowed from fiction—though not classic fiction. Jean-Paul was a lethal vigilante known as Azrael who'd temporarily taken over the mantle of the Batman while Bruce Wayne was recuperating from his near-death battle with Bane. I'd been an avid fan of the Batman comics back when I was a kid, though apparently not quite as avid as Matt Grayson, who had chosen a fitting alias in the charismatic yet mercurial Jean-Paul Valley.

But it wasn't Matt Grayson's alias that Mr. Dorian Gray's finger landed on. It was the far more familiar alias listed below the heading "Viewing Room."

Mr. Gray chuckled as he said, "So, the intrepid young photojournalist is finally unmasked. Pleased to meet you, Mr. Peter Parker . . . or should I say Spider-Man?" He shook his head with a smile of genuine amusement. "You kids with the comic book names. Only us old-timers use the classics anymore. But that's cool. I'm down with it. I had a very memorable evening a couple of weeks ago with the Mighty Thor and his pal Captain Steve Rogers."

I forced a polite smile and nodded, hoping that he wouldn't notice the tension brewing within. It wasn't him. He seemed like a good-natured guy who liked to chat. But the more he chatted, the more I started thinking about what I'd come here for, which clearly wasn't the same thing he'd come for.

His chuckle of delight faded into a nostalgic sigh as he looked at me and said, "My god, you've got beautiful eyes." His expression shifted almost as soon as the words were out of his mouth. "Please don't take offense to that. I'm nothing like Mr. Jean-Paul Valley—not that I have anything against the guy, but . . . " He tapped the entry in the ledger. " . . . you saw him in action last night, so you know what I mean." He gave a short spooky chuckle, followed by a low whistle. "I mean, that guy can be like radioactive intense, am I right? Of course, it's all show—and he's a hellava showman—but a little of that goes a long way, am I right?"

I scarcely nodded. Mr. Gray continued.

"All I'm saying is, I'm not *that* kind of guy. I'm more . . . tame, with a strict 'safe and sane' policy. I mean, I don't mind watching a little rough-and-tumble—who doesn't every now and then, right? I'm just saying that's not my thing . . . unless it's something the other guy is into, you know? I mean, if push comes to shove, and he's really into it, I'll give it a whirl—you only live once, right? But not without ground rules—safety first, right? Unless he's like, 'Hey, anything goes, all-in.' In which case, you don't need ground rules, I suppose. But 'stop' means stop and 'no' means no, and that's when I put the brakes on for sure, you know what I'm saying?"

I nodded again.

He smiled and sighed again. "You're a really good-looking kid. How old are you—if you don't mind me asking?"

"Twenty-seven."

His eyes grew wide, and he stifled a shocked laugh. "Get the fuck outta here." He punched my shoulder lightly. "You look like a *kid*. I was just about to *card* you." He chuckled with delight, and for an odd moment I thought he might actually reach out and muss my hair. But he just shook his head, like he couldn't believe it. "Twenty-seven—you're almost as old as my son!"

I didn't know quite how to respond to that revelation. And luckily I didn't have to, because just then Devon the desk clerk, with his short blond spiky hair and ever-smiling grey-green eyes, appeared. As before, his dimples made a stunning appearance when he spoke. "Welcome back, Mr. Parker."

I looked at him in mild confusion before remembering the entry I'd just seen in the ledger. I hadn't chosen the name "Peter Parker"—in fact, I hadn't given Devon a name at all. But I had a fairly good idea who'd picked this particular alias for me, and in my mind I pictured him standing inside the Sigma, gazing at me with his cool blue eyes and grinning, as if he could see right through the mirrored side of the glass . . . as if he knew precisely who I was and what I was thinking.

Watch watch watch, little Watcher . . . watch watch watch me and learn . . .

I was still picturing Matt Grayson (aka Ponytail, aka Mr. Jean-Paul Valley) capering about in the Sigma from the night before when Devon said, "Your reservation is confirmed, Mr. Parker."

I looked at him with narrowed eyes, and the ghost of a smile played at the corners of his mouth as if the two of us were on the same page—one that Mr. Dorian Gray, who stood next to me, was not privy to. As if to clarify this Devon said, "The Sigma, 7:15 P.M. Your liaison from the art gallery—" He consulted his mobile device. "—MKG, made the arrangements this morning. I trust I am not in error, sir."

I was stunned but quickly recovered and shook my head. "No, you're not."

Once again, Devon's dimples made a winning appearance. "Excellent, sir." When I reached for my wallet, he said, "It's already been taken care of, Mr. Parker. Camden will be along shortly to escort you to your room."

I nodded, but my mind was still reeling a little. I was trying to catch up with all that had transpired over the past few moments when I heard Mr. Dorian Gray inquiring if the Sigma's viewing room was available. Before Devon had the chance to respond, Mr. Gray turned to me and said, "That is, if you don't mind . . . "

Again I froze, and again Devon came to the rescue.

"I'm afraid the viewing room for the Sigma is unavailable this evening, Mr. Gray. A mechanical malfunction. My apologies to you, as well, Mr. Parker."

I nodded, hoping that my sigh of relief looked more like a sigh of disappointment. But Mr. Gray wasn't willing to give up that easily. "Is it the chair? That's no problem. I don't mind sitting in one spot."

My gut clenched, but Devon was unflappable. He offered a polite smile, tinged with appropriate sadness, and said, "I'm afraid it's a little more complicated than that, sir. Once a malfunction is detected, the system locks down the chamber, which can only be opened by the technician. I've placed a call, of course, but regrettably, the technician will not be available until tomorrow morning."

Mr. Gray smiled his on-camera smile, the one that wasn't nearly as genuine as his off-camera smile, and said, "Well, can't you override the system, have one of your guys go down there an open it manually?"

Devon's sad smile returned. "I'm afraid not, sir. Once the system has locked down the chamber, there is no way to gain entry without the technician."

Mr. Gray uttered a short laugh and turned his head to me. "That sucks. What do they do if there's a malfunction while someone is in there? Wait until Monday morning for help to arrive?"

"In the event of an emergency," Devon said, "the chamber can be opened from the inside."

Mr. Gray chuckled and dropped a wink at me. "Too bad someone wasn't in there when it broke down, eh?"

Devon said, "Again, my deepest apologies, sir."

Mr. Gray waved it off with a smile that looked more genuine this time. "No worries." He turned to me again and sighed. "Maybe next time . . . if you're interested?"

I was saved from having to respond this time, when the elevator doors across the lobby swept open and a young man—Camden, I presumed—called out, "This way, sir."

It wasn't until I was inside the elevator with Camden that an odd sensation came over me. I was looking out at the lobby, where Devon stood behind the desk shuffling paperwork while Mr. Gray perused the book of glossy black cards with the Greek symbols on them. The sensation came on suddenly, like a gunshot echoing through a peaceful forest. And in its wake, a single thought floated forward from the back of my mind. A needling thought that I could not suppress: It was as if the entire exchange between Devon and Mr. Gray had been staged specifically to assure me that no one would be watching from the other side of the one-way glass once I entered the Sigma.

I looked out from the opening of the elevator, just in case one of them should happen to offer a telltale glance in my direction. But neither did.

Then the ornate doors slid shut, and the elevator began its swift and steady descent into the depths of The Black Otter.

There was no one to greet us when the elevator doors opened onto the hall with the sleek black floor tiles and chromium walls. As I followed Camden through the labyrinth of corridors, I attempted to memorize the path by counting each turn, but by the time we'd arrived at the door to the Sigma (which, like the viewing room door, blended almost seamlessly into the wall), I wasn't sure I would be able to make it back on my own. I quelled the sliver of panic by reminding myself that if the need to escape arose, I would not be alone. Mickey would be with me. And surely, after being held captive in this place for so long, he would have some knowledge of its corridors—at least enough to guide us back to the elevator.

Unless, the voice of Gordon Powell chimed in suddenly at the back of my mind, *they blindfolded him before bringing him down here, Jack. Or pumped him so full of drugs that he'd be more confused than you. In which case, if push comes to shove, dump the little apple-polisher and make a run for it. He's dead weight, he'll only slow you down. Fuck him. He made his bed, and he can lie in it.*

Part of me wanted to believe this, that Mickey's manipulations—both tender and cruel—had finally caught up with him, and that it was only fitting he should pay the price for his arrogance and vanity. But another part of me—the part where memories still lived of that confused and frightened boy who'd suffered unimaginable horrors—railed against Gordon Powell's cynical judgment.

I was brought back to the moment when Camden waved his hand over the sensor in the wall, and the door to the Sigma opened.

"If you would step into the antechamber, sir, I'll show you how the lock works."

The antechamber was small and dimly lit. Once we were inside with the door shut, Camden instructed me to press my thumb against the small rectangular touchscreen that was mounted to the wall, where the light switch would have been in a normal room. When I pressed my thumb against the little screen, I half expected the lights to go up or down. Instead, the screen lit up blue where my thumb made contact. When I retracted my hand, the image of my thumbprint glowed on the screen, and the words PRINT ACCEPTED appeared in block letters.

I looked at Camden, who remained poised. When the screen went dark, he pressed his thumb against it. The blue scanning light came on again, but this time the words PRINT NOT ACCEPTED appeared below the outline of the thumbprint. Camden waited for the screen to go dark again, then asked me to press my thumb against it. When I did, the panel accepted the print, the tone sounded off, and the door popped open.

Camden explained that once the door was locked, the motion sensor in the hall would no longer be functional (this, he stressed, was to prevent 'accidental intrusion'). He added that the door could only be unlocked by my thumbprint from the inside.

I nodded, but I couldn't suppress the feeling that this

little demonstration was more theatrical than practical. Like the exchange that had occurred between Devon and Mr. Dorian Gray at the front desk, it seemed as if its primary purpose was to convince me that my privacy would be protected and that it was all right to let my guard down, which, of course, I had no intention of doing.

After a brief tutorial on how to use the remote control for the lighting and sound inside the Sigma, Camden stepped into the corridor and turned back to ask, "Has everything been explained to your satisfaction, sir?"

I nodded and thanked him, and when he turned to go, I closed the door and pressed my thumb against the little touchscreen. When the tone sounded off, I went to the opposite side of the antechamber and waved a hand over the sensor. A mild burst of cool air washed over my face as the door to the Sigma slid open. I took a calming breath before crossing the threshold.

When the door closed behind me, I was swallowed in darkness. I held my breath and stood perfectly still. It took a moment, but eventually the sound of steady breathing came from someplace across the room, and I knew that I was not alone.

Though I'd brought the little remote control inside the room with me, I had no intention of turning on any lights. Whether the viewing room was actually locked down and out of commission didn't matter. In a place like The Black Otter, it wasn't difficult to imagine a hidden camera attached to one of the overhead spotlights, and I wasn't about to give anyone who might be watching a crisp bird's-eye view of what I was about to do. I wasn't afraid that keeping the lights off would draw suspicion. I figured that anyone monitoring the room would simply assume that I was one of those shy guys who preferred to do it in the dark.

But keeping prying eyes from intruding would only get me halfway there. For full cover, I would need to block them from *hearing* what was going on in the Sigma as well.

I used the dim light of the remote control's touchscreen to find my way to the jukebox. I combed the entire unit twice in search of the power switch and was ready to give up in exasperation when a sudden thought occurred. I started scrolling through the menu on the little remote control that I'd been using as a makeshift flashlight. I breathed a sigh of relief when the heading "MUSIC" appeared at the bottom of the remote's little screen. I tapped it and found the controls for the jukebox. There was not only a command to turn on the unit, but also settings for its volume, as well as its ornamental lights.

I set the lights at their lowest level and cranked the volume. Then I punched in several of the loudest tunes on the display and waited for the music to start before turning to the shadowy figure of the young man strapped down to the bench at the center of the room.

As I gazed at the outline of his body, scarcely discernible by the bluish-green glow of the jukebox, my heart began to thump like a slow-driving hammer, hellbent on smashing its way out of my chest. I needed to get closer. I needed to remove the oversized blindfold and look into his eyes to know for certain. My paralysis broke, and I stepped forward, toward the naked boy on the bench, as if in a dream.

Just pretend like it's a dream, Mr. M.

Even now, it was difficult to tell if his formal manner of address had been sincere or playful. Either way, with him lying naked beside me in bed, it had certainly had a jarring effect.

We don't have to do anything if you don't want to . . . we can just sleep . . . I just can't be out there alone on the couch . . . not tonight.

It was the same night he'd told me about the waterboarding incident in his basement. He'd been terrified of going home and begged me to let him stay.

It's all right Mr. M. It's not like I'm a kid. I'm graduating *next month. We're almost the same age anyway.*

There was only a four-year age gap between us, but it wasn't all right. It was true that in less than a month he would no longer be my student, but at *that* specific moment, I was still his teacher. Even as he'd reached out and gently closed my eyes with his fingertips, the sane and rational voice in my head had cried out that it was not all right.

We'll just lay here for a while, and if we fall asleep, then there's nothing to worry about . . . and if something more happens, we'll just pretend it's a dream. Either way, it's all good.

But it wasn't all good. There was something more that Mickey wasn't telling me, something hidden beneath that well-polished façade he had constructed. A shadow that extended well beyond anything I could have imagined at the time.

Apple-polisher, the ghost of Gordon Powell whispered in my ear now as I came closer to the naked figure on the bench. My eyes had adjusted to the low light, and I could make out the facial features that were exposed. The smooth line of the jaw, the slight cleft of the chin, the sweet yet sensual lips, the silky shock of blond hair that fell over the top of the blindfold. But it wasn't until I placed a hand on one of his outstretched arms that I knew it was Mickey.

His reaction to my touch was delayed yet decisive. His lips parted as if to speak, but all that came out was a soft moan. Not a moan of pleasure or arousal, but rather the sort of sound one would make in a state of semiconscious confusion. And when I removed the blindfold and looked into his dazed and glassy eyes, I understood why. Whatever he'd been given had been potent enough to sedate him without rendering him unconscious.

My gut clenched and my eyes burned with angry tears as I recalled what I had witnessed from the viewing room the night before.

Could that really have been just last night?

It didn't seem possible that only twenty-four hours ago

I'd sat strapped into the chair in the viewing room, watching Matt Grayson play out his fantasy with my former student.

Mickey had seemed more alert last night than he did now, but he could have been drugged then too. Perhaps they'd given him a bit more tonight since he would be "performing" for a new customer at The Black Otter.

Lounge & Extremities, chimed a needling voice in my head.

But just how extreme? Enough that one of the participants needed to be drugged and tied down to go through with it?

The anger rose like bile, and I fought to choke it back. This was definitely not the time to lose it. I had to keep my head on straight. I had to come up with a plan to get Mickey out of this place.

I was about to say something when Mickey's dazed eyes filled with tears and his lips began to tremble. Everything stopped at that moment, and suddenly it was difficult to breathe. It felt like a knife had pierced my heart when Mickey spoke in a choked whisper.

"I knew you'd find me . . . they said you wouldn't, but I never stopped believing . . . " Tears began to fall down his cheeks as his face contorted into a mask of shame and pain, and his voice cracked like a child's. "I'm sorry, Mr. M. . . . I'm so sorry . . . I screwed up really bad this time, and I can't get out of it . . . there's no way out of it . . . "

His eyes rolled upward, and for a moment I thought he might pass out. I put my hand on his cheek and brushed away the tears with my thumb. I told him to stay with me, that I was going to get him out of this place, that we were going home. For a brief moment, his eyes shined with heartbreaking hope. Then suddenly they looked terrified.

"No," he said in a harsh whisper. *"You've got to get out of here, Mr. M. You've got to go before they find you . . . if they find you here, they'll—"*

"I'm not leaving without you," I said, and before he could protest further, I began to unbuckle the heavy straps that pinned his wrists to the posts at the top of the slanted bench.

He began to moan again, softly, deliriously, as I rubbed his freed arms to get the circulation going. When I stooped to remove the straps from his ankles, his moaning became a little more coherent. "You've got to run, Mr. M. . . . you don't know what they'll do to you if they catch you . . . they're dangerous . . . please run before they find you . . . "

I took off my jacket and wrapped it around Mickey's trembling shoulders. I rubbed his arms again and made him look into my eyes so that he would understand that I was in control now and that he was safe.

"We're leaving here together. Do you understand me?" He nodded. "I'm taking you home, and no one is going to stop me. Do you trust me?" He nodded again. "I need you to stand up now and come with me. I'm not going to let anyone hurt you. Do you understand that?"

The tears began to spill again, and as he wrapped his arms around me, strangled sobs shook his body. I held him tightly and stroked the back of his head while whispering that it was all right, that everything was going to be all right, that he was safe now. I kept repeating it over and over, not sure if it was Mickey or me that I was trying to convince, and finally he relaxed enough that I was able to get him moving toward the door. We hadn't taken more than a few steps when I discovered just how wrong I was.

In a sudden flash, harsh light filled the room from every angle, blinding me. Before my eyes had the chance to adjust to the bright lights, the airlock-like sound of the door whooshing open cut through the loud music coming from the jukebox's speakers, and rapid footfalls on the tiled floor followed. Shadows of as many as five figures came straight at us. I tried to step in front of Mickey to protect him, but while two of the intruders pushed passed me to get to Mickey, the other three grabbed me—one from behind, with his powerful arm wrapped around my throat, while the others each took firm hold of my arms.

My vision returned in time for me to see Mickey being forced back onto the slanted bench by the two young men who'd brushed past me, and that's when I began to struggle violently against the three who'd taken hold of me. I'm not exactly sure of the words that came out, but I was yelling at them with all the force I could muster until the one behind me tightened his choke hold against my windpipe.

Mickey struggled against the men who held him down, and he screamed, "*Please don't hurt him! He doesn't know anything! You can let him go, he doesn't know anything! Tell them, Mr. M., please tell them you don't know anything!*"

As Mickey's hoarse plea was drowned out by the pulsing dance beat coming from the jukebox, a familiar figure entered the room. He was dressed as he had been the night before, in an expensive suit, with long auburn hair pulled back into a ponytail. He surveyed the scene with his calm blue eyes, then turned to me and said, "We'll see what you know, Jack."

I was dragged backward through the antechamber, out into the hall, and through another door directly opposite the Sigma. There were more men waiting in this room, and they helped the others to hoist me onto a table and strap me down.

The room was brightly lit, like an operating theater in a hospital. As I gazed into the harsh light above the table, my heart began to slam in a slow driving beat, and a cold sweat broke out over my body. I struggled to keep myself calm and focused as I choked out a warning: "People know that I'm here . . . I left a note in my apartment . . . detailing everything that's happened over the past few weeks."

Matt Grayson leaned in over me, cutting off the light from directly above, and smiled a small smile. "No you didn't, Jack," he said calmly. "We've been to your apartment, and we didn't find anything there." His smile deepened and his eyes shined. "We're very thorough about these things."

He took off his jacket and handed it to one of the young men. Then he rolled up his sleeves and said, "You don't need to worry. We have no intention of harming you . . . or Mickey for that matter. In fact, when all of this is over, you may take your former student wherever you like. I'll open the front door for you myself. But first, I need you to answer a few questions. And then I need you to do a tiny favor for me, one that won't even cause you to break a sweat. OK?"

Despite his pleasant tone, I tensed when he unbuttoned the left cuff of my shirt and rolled the sleeve above the crook of my arm. I felt a powerful set of hands press down on my shoulders when Matt Grayson took a rubber strap and cinched it around my upper arm.

"Steady, Jack," he said, as he took a hypodermic syringe from the tray beside the table and filled it with clear liquid from a vial. "This is only going to take a moment, and you'll scarcely feel the prick."

He shot a short stream of liquid into the air, then tapped my arm to raise a vein. My heart began to beat faster. The hands on my shoulders pressed down firmly. Matt Grayson administered the injection like a skilled doctor. There was nothing I could do to stop it.

"There we are," he said as he set the syringe back on the tray. "Now relax and don't try to fight it. That will only prove a fruitless effort on your part. You're in good hands, Jack. Nobody is going to hurt you. You have my word."

I did try to fight it, but he was right. It was a fruitless effort. It came on swiftly, but instead of putting me out, as I'd fully expected it to do, it simply left me hovering in a half-conscious sort of limbo. A nice and cozy state that felt warm and secure, despite my predicament.

I had just enough time to wonder if this was the same drug they'd given Mickey when Matt Grayson smiled down at me and said, "Feels nice, eh? Not a worry in the world on this smooth ride, teacher man. Like floating on a cloud."

It was true. I had been transported to a soft fluffy cloud high above in the cool night sky, and it felt very nice. Like I could just stay there forever and never have to worry about anything again. I was dimly aware of Matt Grayson's gentle hands removing my tie and unbuttoning my shirt. Then the even gentler sensation of his fingertips caressing my chest and stomach, moving down toward the waist of my trousers, slipping in for a little look-see . . . or a little touch-feel . . . which made me smile because something was definitely going on down there. I looked around from my cloud to see if maybe I might be able to spot Mickey floating by on *his* cloud, or perhaps lounging on the lower curve of the slivered moon. But I was all alone on this wondrous flight from the real world far below.

I was still tingling with his gentle touch when Matt Grayson retracted his hand from my trousers and said, "He's clean."

Then he was speaking to me again, and when I looked up with my slow-motion eyes, I could see his face close to mine. He was smiling a sweet smile, and I knew that he liked me and meant me no harm because he was stroking my hair and smiling and telling me what a good boy I was. He said he needed me to focus and concentrate for him. He said it was very important and asked me if I could do that for him. I wanted to tell him that I would do *anything* for him because he was speaking so nicely and gently and not messing with this incredible high I was on. But all I could manage was to nod my head yes.

Matt Grayson's smile deepened, and in turn, my smile deepened because he was like my mirror, because we had both done naughty things with Mickey (though he had gone much farther than I), and it's hard not to smile back when your reflection is smiling at you.

"Do you remember Gordon Powell?" he asked.

I nodded because I did. Gordon Powell was the old guy who'd taught art at the high school where I taught English and drama. Gordon was dead because he'd smoked too many hollow-points, which were cigarettes, which were bad for you because they make you cough and make it hard for you to breathe and eventually give you cancer or emphysema or a heart attack, which was what killed Gordon.

I was about to add that, in addition to teaching and smoking, Gordon also painted naughty pictures of naked boys, and that he did this under a fake name and then sold the paintings and bought them back for more money than he'd sold them for. But Matt Grayson was asking me something else now. Something about an otter, which made me laugh because otters are funny.

Matt Grayson smiled and nodded as if to say that he thought otters were pretty funny too. Then he said, "But I need to know, did Gordon ever talk to you about The Black Otter? Did he ever say anything to you about this place? Or talk about any of the people he'd seen here?"

This time I got it. He wasn't talking about the funny kind of otters, which were cute and cuddly and liked to show off when they knew you were watching. He was talking about the *other* kind of otter. *The Black Otter—Lounge and Extremities,* which was a spooky mansion on a wooded hill where *people* liked to show off when they knew you were watching. But there was nothing cute and cuddly about the performances they gave in the sub level chambers.

I shook my head in response to his question because Gordon had never mentioned this place to me. I'd only found out about it *after* he'd died, when I'd found the paintings and the matchbook that someone had placed in his apartment for me so that I could find my way here.

I asked Matt Grayson if *he* was that someone. I told him that I wasn't mad about it . . . that I was truly happy about it because if someone hadn't put those things in Gordon's apartment, I never would have found Mickey.

A distant sadness touched Matt Grayson's eyes, and he shook his head. But I wasn't sure what this meant. Was he shaking his head to mean no, it wasn't him who'd put the paintings and the matchbook in Gordon's apartment for me to find my way here to The Black Otter, or no, he didn't know who had done it?

I was about to tell him that I was confused and ask if he would please clarify it for me when someone called out, "Can we please move this along? It's clear he doesn't know anything, so get to the point and tell him what he needs to do for us, for Christ's sake!"

It was an older voice, and it sounded mean, and that scared me, so I stopped smiling. When Matt Grayson turned to speak to the man at the door, I looked up and saw that it was Mr. Dorian Gray from upstairs in the lobby. Only he wasn't wearing his smiling face—not his genuine one, or even the one he used on TV. He looked hard and angry and tired, the way my father used to look when he woke the morning after a hard night of drinking.

I shrunk back and tried to hide behind Matt Grayson because he was friendly and kind and didn't mess with my high, and I was pretty sure that he was strong enough to protect me from Mr. Dorian Gray.

I smiled a secret smile when Mr. Gray backed down to Matt Grayson, who told him that the situation was under control and that if he, Mr. Gray, would relax and stand aside the situation would be resolved. When Matt turned back to me, his face looked a little sad, which in turn made me sad, but he pushed out a small smile and told me that everything was all right.

When I raised my head and whispered "Mr. Gray scares me," Matt nodded and whispered back, "He scares me a little too."

This surprised me because I didn't think *anything* scared Matt Grayson—he was, after all, the indomitable Jean-Paul Valley, a fearless knight of vengeance and retribution, and up until this moment, I'd assumed *he* was the one in charge here.

He leaned in a little close, and I craned my neck so that our faces were even closer. I mirrored his serious expression as I listened intently to what he had to say.

"I'm going to help you out here, Jack, but I need you to help me too. Do you understand?"

I nodded, and he took a short breath before going on.

"Do you remember the key that came in the card this morning?"

I nodded again because I did remember it. It was a flat brass key that looked like it fit into a very special lock. I told him this, and he nodded with a grave expression.

"That's right, Jack. It's a key for a very special lock. So special that you're the only one who can open it."

"No," I said in a stunned tone of voice, which for some reason made Matt Grayson smile as if I'd said something funny. It didn't seem funny to me, but I smiled back at him because I didn't like to see him sad and it made me happy to see him smile again.

"Yes," he said. "It's a special key to a special lock that only you can open. Did you notice the numbers engraved in the key? Those numbers correspond to a box inside a bank, and the only people who can get at that box are Gordon Powell and you."

"But Gordon's dead," I said.

"I know that," he said. "But luckily he had the foresight to put your name down at the bank so that in the event of his death, the box could still be opened."

"He was really smart," I said, with a serious nod.

"That he was," Matt Grayson said.

"Because, if he didn't put someone's name down, the box could never be opened again," I said.

I was shaking my head, marveling over how ingenious Gordon had been, when Mr. Gray groaned from his place near the door and said, "How much of that shit did you give him? He's so fucked up, he'll never be able to remember what to do when he comes down! Fucking Christ, what the hell kind of operation are you guys running here?"

"Calm down," Matt Grayson called over his shoulder.

"*You* calm down, this is my fucking political life we're talking about here—and the lives of a lot of other decent people as well."

Matt Grayson gave a short laugh that didn't sound much like a laugh at all and said, "Is that what we are now, Mr. Gray—decent?"

"Oh fuck you, Valley," Mr. Gray said with vehemence. "Not all of us are into those sick little perverted games you get off on."

"Not too sick to strap in and watch, though, right?"

Mr. Gray's deeply tanned face went almost red. "You listen, you son of a bitch—"

He was cut off by a voice calling from the corridor outside the room. An oddly familiar voice that at once was diminished by the distance yet filled with authority.

"Mr. Gray," the disembodied voice called out, like a teacher summoning an errant pupil. The effect was instantaneous. Mr. Gray glared at Matt Grayson, then turned and left the room without another word.

I was still puzzling over that voice from the corridor, telling myself that it couldn't possibly be who I'd thought it was, when Matt Grayson turned back to me and said, "I need you to listen to me, Jack, all right? We don't have much time here. Do you understand?"

I nodded because his expression looked very grave. He leaned in closer, as if to prevent the others from hearing what he had to say.

"I'm not in control here. I just do my job and don't ask any questions. And right now, this is my job. I need you to take the key to the bank and bring me the contents of the box. Everything you find in it, no matter how insignificant its appearance. You need to bring the contents of the box to me here, no later than tomorrow evening. Do you understand?"

I was frozen because Matt Grayson's grave expression was scaring me now. I wanted him to smile and laugh like before. But his expression didn't change.

He pitched his voice lower and said, "I can protect Mickey and assure you that no harm will come to him over the next twenty-four hours, but if you don't bring me the contents of that box by tomorrow night at this time, these guys are going to get antsy . . . and when that happens, I won't be able to stop them from doing things to Mickey . . . things that can't be undone. Do you understand that, Jack?"

I did understand. Because I knew all about things that couldn't be undone. I knew the terrible things that Mickey's father had done to him, and I knew that those things could never be undone. But as I looked into Matt Grayson's uncomplicated eyes, I got the feeling that the things *his* people could do would make the things Mickey's father had done seem like charitable acts of mercy by comparison.

To confirm my unspoken suspicion, Matt Grayson added, "There won't be any grace period or warning, Jack. They'll simply remove Mickey from the equation, and then find someone else that you care about."

But there wasn't anyone else, I thought. Aside from Gordon and my mother, who were both dead, Mickey was the closest thing to family that I had. My stomach twisted a little at the thought, but it was true.

As if reading my thoughts, Matt Grayson shook his head sadly and said, "Trust me, Jack, they'll find someone else that you do care about—someone you possibly don't even know that you care about—and they'll make him suffer until you get them what they want."

I still couldn't think of anyone other than Mickey, but that didn't matter. Mickey's safety mattered more than enough to motivate me. I nodded and said, "I'll do it."

Matt Grayson released a breath through his nose that would have seemed like a sigh of relief coming from just about anyone else, and said, "Good man."

My mind was still whirring from the incredible high I was on, even though it had already crested and begun its steady descent into the downward spiral. I laid my head back on the table and closed my eyes against the white light above. I was so exhausted that I scarcely felt the prick of the second needle. When I opened my eyes, Matt Grayson was still there. He was smiling sadly again, which made me smile sadly too.

The last thing I saw was someone handing my jacket to Matt, and Matt slipping a folded sheet of paper into the breast pocket. After that, my eyelids closed and all was nothing. Save for the sound of the music coming from the jukebox in the Sigma room across the hall. Not one of the pulsating tunes I'd punched into the juke's key panel to cover up the sound of my failed attempt to rescue Mickey.

No, this one was a slower tune, with a nice mellow tone that lulled me in my seemingly endless descent. And as I drifted, weightless, toward that place where dreams breed and loom larger than life, I suddenly remembered where I'd last heard this particular song.

I'd heard it in my dream. The dream I'd had after the discovery of the matchbook. It was the Pearl Jam song that Gordon had been whistling as we stacked paintings high into the night sky above his roofless apartment. At the time it hadn't seemed terribly significant—it was, after all, just a dream.

But here in the reality of this cold white room beneath The Black Otter, the song seemed to convey a portend.

As I drifted further into the darkness, the lyrics spilled

from the juke's speakers and echoed down the winding pathways of my subconscious mind like a muted warning on repeat . . .

nothing as it seems
nothing as it seems
nothing as it seems

chapter nine

calculation/provocation/revelation

It was just a dream.

I told myself this as I lay with my head half buried in the pillow and gazed at the glowing digits on my alarm clock, while daggers of bright sunlight stabbed through the slits of the blinds over the window.

The whole thing had been nothing more than a dream—the greeting card with the poem and the key; the revelation that Matt Grayson was the model in the second painting; my subsequent trip back to The Black Otter; the meeting with Mr. Dorian Gray at the front desk in the lobby; the discovery of Mickey bound to the bench in the Sigma; the intense scene that followed, in which I had been dragged from the Sigma to the stark white room across the hall. All of it had been one long bad dream.

Some hopeful part of me actually believed this as I watched the digits on my alarm clock turn from 5:59 to 6:00 a.m. That same hopeful part quickly came up with a scenario in which my entire second trip to The Black Otter—Lounge & Extremities had never taken place.

In this alternate version of events, the hopeful voice

within reasoned that when I got out of bed and found my mobile phone, the date would read Sunday, June 1st—not Monday, June 2nd. And this would mean that the night before had been my *first and only* trip to The Black Otter. And further, that all I had witnessed on my one and only visit to that strange mansion in the wooded hills was the kinky show put on by the ponytailed john and the young trick who wasn't Mickey but just someone who happened to *look* like Mickey. *It had to be,* that voice inside insisted, because the alternative was far too frightening to consider.

I didn't have to see the date on my mobile phone to crush the hope within. The evidence that what I'd experienced the night before was in fact *not* a dream greeted me the moment I stepped into the living room.

The painting of Matt Grayson and the painting of the boy in bondage (which I now knew with certainty was Mickey) were both gone. The black matchbook and the greeting card, which I'd left side by side on the coffee table, were gone too. Also missing was Gordon's ledger, which had documented the sales, buy-backs, and resales of numerous paintings, including the two that had been in my possession less than twelve hours ago.

Every tether to The Black Otter had been removed from my apartment, save for one. A single sheet of paper, folded and tucked into the breast pocket of my jacket, which I found draped over the back of a chair in the breakfast nook.

The reality of the situation came home swiftly when I unfolded the sheet of paper and saw the familiar block print, written by the same hand that had printed the Greek symbols on the inside flap of the matchbook, as well as the poem inside the greeting card. Only here on this plain sheet of paper, the message wasn't even remotely mysterious. No Greek symbols. No cryptic nineteenth-century verse. Just an address.

My focus shifted from the sheet of paper to the flat brass key on the tray at the center of the breakfast table. I hadn't put it there. I'd taken it with me to The Black Otter and left it in the pocket of my jacket. As I gazed at the key now, I could hear Matt Grayson speaking to me softly in the white room across the hall from the Sigma.

It's a special key to a special lock that only you can open. Did you notice the numbers engraved in the key? Those numbers correspond to a box inside a bank, and the only people who can get at that box are Gordon Powell and you.

I looked back to the address centered on the sheet of paper while the memory of Matt Grayson's directive continued in that gentle and reasonable tone.

I need you to take the key to the bank and bring me the contents of the box. Everything you find in it, no matter how insignificant its appearance. You need to bring the contents of the box to me here, no later than tomorrow evening. Do you understand?

I understood. But just in case, Matt Grayson had offered a frightening caveat.

. . . if you don't bring me the contents of that box by tomorrow night at this time, these guys are going to get antsy . . . and when that happens, I won't be able to stop them from doing things to Mickey . . . things that can't be undone.

I thought about this warning as I showered and dressed for school. There was no way I could get to the bank before my first class. But I could easily make it on my lunch break. All I had to do was hold it together until noon. Get through my first three classes, and then head downtown for the bank. Once I had the contents of Gordon's safety deposit box in my possession, getting through the rest of the school day would be a breeze. But for now I was focused on making it through the first half of the day, and with my raw nerves and racing mind, this would be no small task.

I had a moment's fright when I stepped outside of my apartment building and didn't see my car in its usual spot. Then it hit me that I wasn't in any condition to drive myself home the night before. The last thing I remembered was the blurry vision of Matt Grayson slipping the sheet of paper into my jacket pocket. After that, my mind was a complete blank. I could only guess that one of the guys from The Black Otter must have driven me home in my car, while someone else (possibly Matt Grayson, aka Mr. Jean-Paul Valley) followed in another car. Then, after tucking me into bed, they'd cleaned the apartment of any evidence linked to The Black Otter and taken off in the second car.

My theory proved correct when I found my car parked around the back side of the building under the shade of a huge willow and close to the rear emergency exit, which could only be opened from the inside. It made sense, as it was the perfect place to act under cover of darkness. I reasoned that the driver of my car had parked back here and waited, with me unconscious in the passenger seat, while the driver of the second car took my keys, entered through the front of the building, and came back to open the emergency door to let us in. From there it would have been relatively easy to get me up to my apartment without being noticed. And even if someone happened to be in the hall or the stairwell, the two guys from The Black Otter would have had no problem explaining that their "friend" had had one too many down at the pub.

The tank was nearly empty (which wasn't surprising, considering my two trips to The Black Otter and back in less than forty-eight hours), so I had to stop off to fill it up, but I made it to school on time. My first two classes went by smoothly and at a surprisingly swift tick. It was finals week, so I didn't have to worry about the normal routine. No teaching, no class discussions. All I had to do was pass out the tests, explain the rules, and leave the students to it.

I'd thought the extended silence would give me too much time to think and worry about all the things that could go wrong—both before *and* after my impending trip to the bank to collect the mysterious contents of Gordon's safety deposit box—but I managed to hold it together remarkably well.

Second period was much easier to get through because I had the tests from the first period class to grade, which helped to distract me, if only to a small degree, from the scary reality that Mickey's safety—possibly even his life—was in my hands.

It wasn't until my third period English class that the façade I'd constructed to get me through the day finally cracked and all the pent-up tension inside broke through like a tidal wave hellbent on destruction.

It came shortly after the final bell with a tentative knock on my open classroom door. It was one of the student assistants from the main office, a plucky girl named Heather Hanover, who was in my sixth period drama class. When I looked up from the paper I was grading, Heather offered an apologetic smile and said, "I'm sorry to interrupt, Mr. M., but Mrs. Derderian sent me . . . from the office. She says that Shane Guerin needs to come down because his father is here to pick him up."

I was about to say something, tell her that we were in the middle of a final here, when I caught sight of Shane sitting in his usual seat at the back of the room. I had been so preoccupied that I hadn't even noticed when he'd entered and taken his seat before the start of class. He had always been a quiet kid at school—the polar opposite of his coffee shop alter ego, Rufus—so there was nothing unusual about him slipping into my classroom unnoticed. Especially on a day like this, when my mind was so preoccupied that all I could think about was running out the clock and getting to the bank. Despite the fact that he was an attractive guy who would have stood out in any crowd, Shane Guerin was surprisingly adept at blending into the background and not being noticed.

But I noticed him now, and my gut clenched as if I'd been sucker-punched. He looked into my eyes for a brief moment and immediately looked down, as if in doing so he might be able to erase what I had seen. Even as his cheeks flushed with shame, the angry purple bruise below his left eye stood out, as if to scream at me *Are you fucking blind, Jack? Didn't you see those bruises on the kid's back when he was changing his shirt in the back room at the coffee shop? Open your eyes!*

My eyes were open. But as I stared at Shane, all I could see was his father, Doug Guerin, standing on the lawn outside of his house the other night. Saturday night. The night when I'd come back from The Black Otter and stopped off for a bite at the coffee shop in the little strip mall off Highway 80. As I stared at the fresh bruise on Shane's cheek, I could feel Doug Guerin's vice grip handshake, and I could hear the warning beneath his words . . .

Can't be too careful with kids running around at night, am I right, Jack?

I could feel his icy blue eyes, much like my own father's eyes, piercing me. I shook my head at my own naïveté. Had I really thought that there wouldn't be consequences for Shane's disobedience? His father had expected him to get a ride with Kaitlin, and accepting a ride from me had been viewed as an act of defiance. And as I well knew from my own upbringing, acts of defiance are always met with swift punishment.

A sickening tremor rose from within as realization dawned on me. At the same time I'd been sitting comfortably on the sofa in my apartment, watching an old video of a former student play acting a moment of emotional torment, this kid with his head down at the back of my classroom had been living real torment. And not just emotional torment. His father had been using him as a human punching bag, under the guise of discipline.

I thought about Shane's reputation for being clumsy, all the scrapes and bruises and broken bones from accidents that conveniently never seemed to happen while he was at school. Always someplace away from school, out of view from his friends and teachers. I thought about the major injury he'd sustained a few years back—the one that had been so bad it kept him out of school long enough that he had to repeat his sophomore year. I thought about his sweet tentative smile and gentle manner—in spite of all that he had endured over the years, I had never once seen a hint of bitterness in his eyes—and I couldn't believe that I had been so blind. How could I have been so attuned to Mickey's personal demons five years ago and not have picked up a single clue to what was going on with Shane in the present?

Because, the voice of Gordon Powell spoke up unexpectedly inside my head, *Mickey* told *you what was going on. He* wanted *your sympathy. He was an apple-polisher, Jack—how many times do I have to tell you this? And* you *were his captive audience. The Guerin boy isn't like Mickey at all. He neither wants nor needs your sympathy. What he wants and needs is to be free of the fray and get on with his life. You saw him at the coffee shop with your own eyes. The kid was a different person there. Open your eyes and breathe, Jack. You've got to get beyond that little apple-polishing prick and take steps here. Let go of the floater and save the one whose head is still above the water. Swim, man, while you still have time to reach him!*

The girl from the office was still standing in the doorway of my classroom. When she called out to me in a tentative tone, I snapped out of my stupor but didn't respond. It wasn't until Shane began to collect his things and place them into his knapsack that I moved.

I stood up and said calmly, "Stay put. Finish the test. Everyone. Back to work. And no talking while I'm gone."

Shane's father saw me coming through the wide glass wall of the main office and broke into a friendly smile before I reached the open door. He was about to extend a hand but stopped short when he saw me up close. His smile faltered for a second, then returned, on full wattage, like a magic trick. Only, his pale blue eyes didn't appear to be in on the act.

"Jack, good to see you again," he said as if we were old acquaintances. "I just came by to pick up my boy."

"I know," I said. "He's in my classroom taking his final. Why don't you give me a message and I'll see that he gets it."

Doug Guerin's features froze in an odd expression. Then the smile returned, and this time it reached his eyes, though there was no humor in it. He leaned in closely and pitched his voice in a pleasant tone. "Tell him his father is here to pick him up."

I met his gaze and said, "I'll let him know as soon as he's finished with his finals. He has three more after lunch, so he won't be done until three o'clock. If you'd like to wait in the teachers' lounge, I'll be more than happy to take you there."

He studied my eyes for a measured moment, then chuckled and said, "I don't know what this is about. I'm just here to pick up my kid—"

"And I just told you he's in the middle of a test."

The muscles in his jaw tensed, and for a second it looked as though he might make a move. Then something in his eyes shifted, and he smiled that humorless smile again. He laughed and clapped his hands together. "You're very good, Jack. I'll give you that. But maybe we should see what the head honcho has to say about this." He kept his gaze on me as he called to the attendants behind the counter, "Would one of you girls be kind enough to ask your principal to join us?"

The girls stood frozen, unsure of what to do. Even Marthe Derderian, the diminutive yet imposing faculty supervisor, was at a loss for words. The tension was broken when Principal Suarez came from her office. She introduced herself and asked if there was a problem.

Shane's father put on his bright smile and said, "Doug

Guerin. Shane's father. No problem at all. I've just come to pick up my son. He's not feeling well. I told him to stay home, but you know how kids are."

Principal Suarez shifted her gaze to me. "Where is the boy now, Mr. McGregor?"

"In my classroom," I said, without taking my eyes off of Doug Guerin.

"Has someone gone up to get him?"

"Yes."

"And is he on his way down here?"

"No, he's not."

Principal Suarez paused, but she didn't look confused. She had been an educator for over twenty years and principal of West High for almost seven more, and even when coming into a situation completely blind, she understood that it was never wise to look confused. She held her gaze for a moment longer and then asked, "Is there a reason why he's not coming down?"

I nodded. "He has finals today. He's taking the exam in my class right now."

Doug Guerin sighed and shook his head as if enduring the protest of a stubborn child. Principal Suarez remained neutral.

"Is he feeling well enough to continue with the exam?" she asked.

"Other than a bruise below his left eye, he seems fine."

Marthe Derderian flinched at the mention of the bruise, a subtle reaction which only I seemed to notice. Principal Suarez looked like a judge pondering evidence. Doug Guerin released a chuckle that came off more like a sigh of disbelief.

"Look," he said, "I've come here to pick up my son. He had an accident this weekend and injured his head. It could be a concussion, we're not sure. But in any case, he's not well enough to be taking tests. He needs to be home in bed where he can rest. Now, I spoke to one of your girls here—"

He turned to a girl behind the desk and asked, "Are you Lydia?"

The girl nodded.

"I spoke to Lydia here," he continued, "and explained that Shane wasn't feeling well and that he would have to make up the exams later. Isn't that right, sweetheart?"

The girl looked frightened, as if she might be in trouble, but managed to nod again.

Doug Guerin's smile returned. "There you have it. Now if you'll send someone up to get my son, we'll be on our way."

Before Principal Suarez could respond, I said, "That's not going to happen."

For a second everyone in the office froze, like figures in a tableau. Then Shane's father said, "Excuse me?"

Principal Suarez was about to interject when I said, "He's not coming down."

Doug Guerin kept his gaze on me as he spoke to Principal Suarez. "Miss Suarez, do I need to remind you that I am Shane's father and legal guardian, and as such, I have the right to take my son out of your school for his own safety."

Marthe Derderian made an abrupt sound that she immediately covered by clearing her throat. Marthe and I had never been allies. In fact, she had been one of the "gang of four"—the group of teachers who had attempted to get me dismissed during my first year at West High. But the contempt in her small dark eyes as she gazed at Shane's father gave me the feeling that she and I were finally on the same page, at least on this one issue.

My feeling was confirmed when she casually posited a reasonable counter to Doug Guerin's argument. "Shane is nineteen . . . "

Principal Suarez looked at Marthe, then back to Shane's father, and said, "If the student is no longer a minor, I'm afraid I can't help you, Mr. Guerin."

His features froze in a mildly quizzical expression, as if he half expected the principal to break into a smile and tell him that she was only kidding and that she would send someone up to get his son at once. But Principal Suarez wasn't joking, and though he smiled at her and offered cordial nods to the others behind the main desk, Doug Guerin wasn't amused.

He turned to go but stopped short of the door. He leaned in close to me and spoke softly as he looked into my eyes. "Are we drawing the line here, Jack? Is that what this is? Because I'm very good at drawing lines, and I know how to handle young punks who cross those lines. So you might want to ask yourself one question: 'Do I *really* want to do this?'" He paused and leaned in closer. "A little something you should know about me, son: I don't take well to being publicly humiliated. Believe it or not, when push comes to shove, I can be a real prick."

I remained silent, waiting for him to make a move, anything that would give me reasonable cause in the eyes of the witnesses behind the main desk. A pat on the arm or shoulder, anything that could be interpreted as an act of aggression.

But instead, he smiled and said, "You don't want to tangle with the big bull, Jack. You'll mess up that pretty face of yours. And then none of the little schoolboys will want you."

It would have ended right there, with a stinging shot across the bow that cut even deeper than he could have imagined. But Doug Guerin wanted more, and he got it when he leaned in closer, his lips almost touching my ear, and whispered, "I know your weakness, Jack. Because you wear it on your sleeve. You think you can save these kids, but you can't save them all. I've got the one who's got your heart, and your little triumph here is a hollow victory, because once he comes home—and, trust me, he's got no other place to go, because I'm all he's got, and he knows it—I'm gonna make him pay for your arrogance. And this time there won't be a visible mark on him—I'm very proficient at what I do, just ask my former CO at Bagram. You fucked with the wrong guy, kemosabe, and I can assure you that the consequences will be dire."

He pulled back from my ear and broke into a convincing friendly grin as he pierced me with his pale blue gaze. "Now, ask yourself, Jack, do I look like I'm lying?"

I don't remember him turning and walking away. I don't remember following him into the hall. And I don't remember the point of contact. All I remember from that protracted moment of blinding rage was me holding the collar of his shirt in one tightly clenched fist while punching him repeatedly with my other fist until my vision blurred into shades of fiery red and impenetrable black.

When I finally came back to myself, the school security guards had a hold of me, and one of them was saying, "Easy, Jack, easy." And my chest was heaving, and I was panting as I gazed at Doug Guerin through the sweaty veil of my bangs. But I could see him clearly. He was sprawled on the hallway floor, but his eyes were open, and he was smiling at me through his bloody and swollen face as if he were the victor.

It wasn't until I was sitting in a holding cell at the police station, staring down at my bloody knuckles, that realization dawned on me.

And by then, it was all but too late.

I'd been in the holding cell for three hours when a guard came and unlocked the door. At first I thought I was being moved to a different cell, or possibly even another facility, and so I was surprised when the guard led me down a hallway and left me alone at the window of a small office. The officer behind the window asked for my name, and when I gave it to him, he placed a large envelope on the counter and told me to make sure that all of my personal effects were inside. The envelope contained my phone, my tie, my shoelaces, and my wallet. Then the officer slid a clipboard across the counter and asked me to sign at the bottom of the sheet. Then he took back the clipboard and told me I was free to go.

The officer went back to his paperwork, and I stood at the little counter with a confused expression until he pointed a finger toward the far end of the hall. "It's down there and to the left." When I still didn't move, he said, "Is there something I can help you with?"

I hesitated again and then forced myself to speak. "Can you tell me who posted my bail?"

"No bail," he said, without looking up from his paperwork. "Your buddy dropped the charges. You're free to go, slugger."

When I stepped outside and saw my car parked across the street from the police station, the fog of confusion began to lift. When I found the note tucked under the driver's side wiper blade, all confusion evaporated.

The note was written in neat block letters on the back of a pink flyer announcing:

YOUR FUTURE
YOUR AMBITION
YOUR ACCOUNT

APPLY AT ANY BRANCH TODAY!

I didn't have to flip the flyer over to know what the message was about or who it was from, but I did anyway. It read:

YOU'RE WELCOME, JACK.

And that was all. When I flipped it back to the front, I noticed that the bank's closing hour for weekdays was circled in the same ink that was used to write the note on the back. 5:00 P.M.

The bank was nearby, but I was pretty sure that a guy in a bloodstained shirt would throw up more than a few flags, and right now I wasn't looking to draw any more attention to myself. By my phone's clock, it was 2:30. More than enough time to go home and get cleaned up before the bank closed.

I was back in my apartment and standing under the warm downpour from the showerhead when several realizations came crashing down on me in rapid succession.

The first and most glaring was that someone at The Black Otter had been watching me closely enough to know that I had been arrested for assaulting the parent of one of my students at school—and whoever that someone was had paid a visit to Doug Guerin and convinced him to drop the charges. It wasn't difficult to believe that the someone in question had been Matt Grayson, and that possibly he'd brought a few of the boys along to ensure that Doug Guerin would understand the gravity of the situation. Shane's father was a spooky man, but Matt Grayson and his entourage from The Black Otter were spookier. And if Mr. Dorian Gray was any indication of their "extended associates," they were extremely well-connected in high places. It was possible that they had appealed to Doug Guerin with reason, and maybe even offered him a payoff for his trouble. But it was more likely that Matt Grayson had simply recognized the bully and used the tactic that all bullies are susceptible to: the bigger bully. The one who has no compunction about going too far, the one who does not fear that his handiwork will be seen, the one who derives no pleasure from the pain and fear of his victims, the one whose sole purpose is to produce the tangible results at any and all costs. It was more likely that Doug Guerin had stared into the uncompromising eyes of Matt Grayson and quickly come to the realization that far more than his wounded pride was on the line.

The second thing to hit me was of less concern—at least

in the heat of the moment, with far more pressing matters on my mind. Regardless of Doug Guerin's change of heart on pursuing the assault and battery charge, I was very likely out of a job. Even with Principal Suarez, and possibly even Marthe Derderian, standing up to speak on my behalf, the security camera video footage of me violently attacking a parent on school grounds would certainly be more than enough to sway the majority of school board members to vote for my dismissal.

The third was more of a feeling than a realization. Above and beyond all of the strange events and disturbing discoveries that had occurred since I'd come across the painting and the matchbook in Gordon's apartment—those tantalizing clues that had ensured my involvement—I couldn't get over the feeling that I had been manipulated into this position. And that the seeds of deception had been planted long before Gordon's death. Not in preparation for this particular outcome, but more by way of a fortuitous twist of fate.

As the warm water continued to spill over my head, across my shoulders, and down my back and legs, I could hear voices from the past and present coming together, like pieces of a puzzle sliding into place . . .

I'm sorry about this, Mr. M. I just needed a place to unwind—my dad's on the warpath again.

Can't be too careful with kids running around at night, am I right, Jack?

Could I crash here tonight? Just tonight. Things'll be better tomorrow, and I'll go home, I promise.

Next time you need a ride to school after you've been out all night, you call me . . . I will not be publicly humiliated.

He does these things to me, Mr. M.—

I'm very proficient at what I do . . .

—things that he used to do when he was in Afghanistan.

. . . just ask my former CO at Bagram.

His eyes . . . like the eyes of those white wolves . . . I swear it, Mr. M.

Don't let me hear that you've been with that boy again.

Please, Mr. M., just let me crash here for tonight, I swear it'll be the last time.

I know your weakness, Jack.

We don't have to do anything if you don't want to . . . we can just sleep . . .

Once he comes home—and, trust me, he's got no other place to go, because I'm all he's got, and he knows it—I'm gonna make him pay.

Please, Mr. M.

And this time there won't be a visible mark on him.

I knew you'd find me . . . they said you wouldn't, but I never stopped believing . . .

You think you can save these kids, but you can't save them all.

I clenched my hands into fists against the slick tiled wall of the shower as the intersecting voices from the past and present faded and only the distant promises and warnings of my two former students, Mickey Greenleaf and Marilyn Plath, remained . . .

Thanks for believing in me . . .

You don't know him, Mr. McGregor.

I'm going to make you so proud . . .

Get away from him while you still can.

Wait and see, things will be different when I come back.

He's gonna break your heart the same way he did mine.

Just pretend like it's all a dream, Mr. M.

I clenched my fists tighter and spit water as one final voice from the past weighed in with sagacious wisdom:

The boy is an apple-polisher, Jack. Plain and simple.

By this point, the water had begun to run cold. But I forced myself to stay there until the chilly downpour numbed every nerve in my trembling body. The puzzle still wasn't complete, but enough pieces had fallen into place to convince me what my next move needed to be.

I got dressed quickly and wrapped the raw knuckles of my left hand in gauze. I got to the bank with an hour to spare before closing. I'd assumed there would be more of a procedure, but Gordon's key and my ID were all I needed to gain access to the vault. The attendant left me alone with the box in a small room adjacent to the vault and told me to press the buzzer next to the door when I was finished.

I took a short breath before twisting the little latch on top of the box. Then I exhaled with resignation and opened the lid. Though I wasn't exactly surprised by the contents, I was more than a little shocked at the amount. Over forty packets of one hundred dollar bills, each neatly stacked and wrapped in crisp white bands that read: $10,000.

As I gazed down at that money, I didn't feel the elation that people do in movies or TV shows when they stumble upon a fortune in cash. I didn't smile with glee, and I didn't jump for joy. I just stood there nonplussed until the sinking sensation inside caught up with the rest of me. And then I released a sigh and thought *My god, Gordon, what were you involved in?*

No answer came back—not even one of the cryptic sort Gordon had offered up freely as we'd climbed the staircase of paintings in my dreams.

But this wasn't a dream. It was real. And Gordon was no longer able to provide answers, cryptic or otherwise.

I thought about the paintings—in particular, the one of the boy in bondage that according to the entries in Gordon's ledger had been sold and bought back—and suddenly the notion that Gordon might have been involved in an art scam seemed to have real credence. But what could that possibly have to do with The Black Otter? Other than the obvious fact that the painting had been done inside the Sigma, the connection seemed too threadbare. And if Gordon had been involved in an art scam that had paid off as handsomely as the stash in his bank box indicated, why wasn't his ledger filled with numerous sales and buy backs? Surely he couldn't have made all this money off of a single scam?

It was then that Gordon spoke clearly inside my head.

Not the ghost of Gordon, nor a dream induced incarnation, but the real Gordon, speaking to me in the teachers' lounge a few years back.

There are no real mysteries amongst men, Jack. All those complex layers and intricacies are merely subterfuge, laid down by small minds attempting to think big. When you cut a path through all of the man-made minutiae and get down to the core truth, you'll find it's quite simple and straightforward. "I did it for love, I did it for money, I did it for revenge, I did it for fame . . . " Take your pick, it's all the same rudimentary crap. You can take the animal out of the jungle, stick him in a suit, trim his hair, and teach him to stand up on two legs, but in the end, he's still an animal, and, as such, his motive—his core truth—will always be simple . . . even when things appear less than transparent.

He'd smiled at me through the stream of smoke that trailed up from the tip of his cigarette like an uncoiling viper waiting to strike its master, and said, *Cheer up, Jack. You and I are likely the only people in this entire school who actually understand the simple truth behind the machinations of the human animal, and that gives us the edge: We can see him coming, long before he gets the first wall of his maze built.*

Gordon had been wrong about that one. I hadn't possessed the ability to see through the complex layers that others were capable of constructing in order to shield their simple core truths.

But I was starting to see now, and I was fairly certain that Gordon had never written that second entry in his ledger, the one that indicated the buy-back of the painting of the boy in bondage. Someone else had written it. The same person who had placed the painting of the boy in bondage in Gordon's apartment, along with the matchbook.

Subterfuge, Jack, the voice of Gordon Powell chimed inside my head. *Peel away that muck, and you find the simple truth beneath.*

I'd emptied my gym bag back at the apartment and

brought it along, just in case, and now I stacked all forty-three bricks of cash into the bag, with little room to spare. I was zipping the bag shut when I noticed there was something else in the box. It sat in the darkened space at the back corner, so small that I might have missed it, had the light from above not hit it at just the right angle. I reached inside, took it out, and stared at it with curiosity. It was a memory stick. Plain and black, a generic brand you could pick up at just about any shop with an electronics department. As I turned it over between my fingers, I could hear Matt Grayson's voice cutting through the haze while I lay strapped down to the table in the white room across the hall from the Sigma.

I need you to take the key to the bank and bring me the contents of the box. Everything you find in it, no matter how insignificant its appearance.

The idea that a memory stick could be of equal or greater value to all the cash I'd just loaded into my gym bag seemed a bit absurd, but something told me that an absurdity of that order would fall right in line with the goings on at an establishment like The Black Otter—Lounge & Extremities. And if so, this little memory stick might be the only bargaining chip I had to play when it came down to the clutch.

I put the stick in my pocket and rang for the attendant to let me out. But I didn't head for the highway, because there was one more stop I needed to make before making that long trip up north.

I had my suspicions—more than enough to convince just about anyone *but* me—but I needed confirmation. I needed to know beyond all doubt that what I suspected was in fact that simple truth that Gordon had spoken of. I needed to know what I was about to encounter on my final visit to The Black Otter.

. . .

It was quarter to five when I pulled up to the little white house with the neatly trimmed hedges bordering the lawn and the bright flowering shrubs that adorned the beds of soil on either side of the porch. Mickey's mother greeted me with a smile at the screen door and invited me in as if I were an old family friend. She was older than I'd imagined, old enough in fact to be Mickey's grandmother, but her gait was like that of a woman twenty years her junior. She was happy to finally meet "Michael's favorite teacher" after all the years of hearing such wonderful things about "the awesome Mr. M." And she was extremely grateful for all that I'd done to help her son "reach his potential and see his dreams come true."

At first I was completely lost. She was speaking as if Mickey had achieved his dream of making it big on Broadway, and not at all as if he'd gotten no further than Pierpoint, Pennsylvania. My confusion evaporated and was replaced by a bitter sense of understanding when she showed me the playbills Mickey had sent her from New York. They were all very professional-looking, with titles of actual shows that had run on Broadway, like *Red* and *Equus* and *The History Boys*. The playbills looked so authentic that were it not for the fact that the names of the lead actors who'd actually appeared in all of these shows had been removed and replaced by Mickey's name, I would have sworn they were genuine Broadway programs. He had even sent her scripts from some of his hit shows, autographed by his "co-stars" (real actors like Richard Griffiths and Alfred Molina).

She told me how she had wanted to go to New York and see Mickey perform, but Mickey didn't want her leaving his father in the care of strangers. "He's always been so considerate of his dad," she said with a gleam of genuine pride in her misty eyes as she looked down at the phony play bill for *The History Boys*. "Oh, it broke Michael's heart to leave him.

I don't believe there's ever been a more devoted son." She smiled a knowing motherly smile and confided, "He loves us both equally, but I've always known that he holds a special place in his heart for his dad. They say that the bond between mother and son is the strongest, but they never saw Michael and his father together."

I sat in stunned silence. Despite my growing suspicions about Mickey's purported volatile relationship with his father, hearing his mother speak of the unbreakable bond between her husband and son was jarring, to say the least.

Even more jarring was meeting Mickey's father face to face.

He had been up for his afternoon nap when I'd arrived, but shortly after Mickey's mother put on the tea kettle in the kitchen, he came down the back stairwell, aided by a dark-haired woman in her late thirties. The trip down the last four steps that were visible from the kitchen table was long and hard fought, but Mickey's father, who looked a good ten years older than his wife, smiled through the pain and thanked the younger woman as she handed him his canes. He made his way to the table in the same slow fashion, and when he finally eased down into the chair opposite me, he dropped a wink and said, "Just like British Rail. We may be late, but we get there."

As I sipped tea that smelled faintly of cinnamon and cloves, I tried to reconcile the image of the domineering and brutal patriarch that Mickey had planted in my mind with the frail man seated across the table from me. I even briefly entertained the idea that the accident or disease which had claimed the mobility of this soft-spoken man had been a recent event, and that before then he had been every ounce the ruthless tyrant Mickey spoke of with such convincing passion. But deep down I knew better. And after tea, Mickey's mother unwittingly presented me with the irrefutable proof I'd come for.

While the old man retired to the family room to watch

the early evening news, Mickey's mother took me upstairs to her son's old room, which she had lovingly kept preserved like a time capsule. She brought me there to show me other things Mickey had sent her from New York. Photographs of Mickey with famous people, posters of his plays, glossy booklets, all meticulous mock-ups that even a trained eye would have had trouble spotting as forgeries—most impressive among them, a perfect replica of the Drama Desk Award with Mickey's name engraved on it. Looking at the trophy, which held a prominent place on the shelf with Mickey's high school awards, I couldn't help feeling a grudging respect for his restraint—at least he hadn't had the temerity to fake winning a Tony Award.

By far, the largest section of the puzzle came into view while we were looking at photographs Mickey had sent from New York. Mrs. Greenleaf had temporarily housed the newest photos in one of Mickey's old albums ("Just until I have a chance to pick up a new one—there's a lovely shop in Pittsburgh that has these wonderful cloth-bound scrapbooks, but I don't get up that way as often as I used to."), so as she flipped through pages, the doctored photos of Mickey with celebrities in New York were interspersed with real photos of Mickey back in high school. She was just about to turn a page on one of these older images when my hand shot forward gently to stop her. I tried to look casual as the blood pounded at my temples in near-dizzying waves.

"Who is that with Mickey?" I asked, even though I already knew. The boy in the photograph was slightly taller than Mickey, though clearly younger by at least three years—*Four, to be exact,* a voice inside my throbbing head amended. The two of them, Mickey and this boy, were at what appeared to be a pool party. They stood side by side, smiling for the camera, their hair wet and their bare chests and shoulders dappled with water, as if they just come from the pool. While the younger boy's physique was nowhere near the level of Mickey's, his shoulders were broad and, at fourteen, he'd already begun to develop lines of definition.

"That's the Guerin boy," Mickey's mother said, with an affectionate smile. "Michael and he had become very close. I believe he was a freshman when Michael was a senior. They met on the swim team, and Michael sort of took Shane under his wing. Such a sweet boy. Very polite and very quiet. But Michael could get him to come out of his shell and open up. He trusted Michael and looked up to him like a big brother. Michael always had the gift of making others feel special, and I believe that was something Shane really needed." She offered a sad smile and confided, "I don't think he had a very good home life. His mother died when he was younger, and his father seemed a bit on the cold side—though I only met him once, when he came here to pick up Shane, so I shouldn't really judge."

I offered an understanding nod, but inside it was as if I were trapped in a dream from which I could not wake, as if I had been plunged into a depthless pool and no matter how hard I struggled I could not get back to the surface. And from that depthless pool, I could hear those familiar voices again . . .

I'm sorry about this, Mr. M. I just needed a place to unwind—my dad's on the warpath again.

Can't be too careful with kids running around at night, am I right, Jack?

Could I crash here tonight? Just tonight. Things'll be better tomorrow, and I'll go home, I promise.

Next time you need a ride to school after you've been out all night, you call me . . .

He does these things to me, Mr. M.—

I'm very proficient at what I do . . .

His eyes . . . like the eyes of those white wolves . . . I swear it, Mr. M.

Don't let me hear that you've been with that boy again.

All of those stories Mickey had told me about the abusive father were true. Only they weren't *his* stories to tell. He had stolen them from Shane. He had taken a frighten and abused freshman under his wing and used the horror stories the boy had told him—real stories of actual abuse—to gain my sympathy and trust. And he had done it with such convincing ease, as if it were as natural as breathing.

I told you, Jack, the voice of Gordon Powell chimed in suddenly, *the boy is an apple-polisher. Plain and simple.*

In my mind, I pictured Mickey standing on the surface of the water, looking down at me, ready to place the sole of his foot on my head and shove me back under the moment I made it through to catch a breath.

I snapped out of my reverie when Mickey's mother spoke again. She was looking down at the photo of Mickey and Shane at the poolside with the sun shining down on them when she said with a sigh, "I'm glad that Michael was there for him."

But Mickey hadn't been there for Shane. Shane had trusted Mickey enough to confide his deepest and darkest secret, and Mickey had done nothing to help him. He had taken what he could get from the boy and left him adrift in a nightmare that had continued up to this very day.

I felt the sudden urge to shout this at the old woman sitting on the bed next to me, but when she looked up from the photo with tears brimming in her eyes, I simply nodded with a reassuring smile and told her that Mickey had done a good job as a friend, that Shane was graduating this year and would be heading off to college in the fall. She was genuinely heartened to hear that Shane was doing well.

After a brief goodbye to Mickey's father, who was still watching television in the family room, I turned to Mickey's mother at the front door and asked a question to which I already knew the answer. "If you don't mind, may I ask, was your husband ever in the service?"

"Oh my, no," she said with the air of one grateful for the change of subject. "Gerald never served in the military. He was diagnosed with CP when he was five."

"I'm sorry," I said.

She waved it off with a smile. "He manages well, as you can see."

"Yes, he does," I said with a nod and smile. "Thank you for having me in your home."

"Not at all, thank you for stopping by. It was so nice to finally meet you after all this time." She gave a motherly sigh, mixed with a weary laugh. "I'm sure Michael would have been mortified at you meeting us back when he was still in your class, but he's all grown up now, so I'm sure he wouldn't mind you stopping by for a visit."

I nodded again, but as I headed down the path I had the distinct feeling that Mickey wouldn't have approved of this little visit with his parents at all. And as I backed out of the driveway and headed for the highway, I realized that I couldn't have cared less what Mickey thought. The only thing I cared about now was getting to The Black Otter as quickly as possible and making the trade-off. What Mickey did after I got him out of the jam he'd got himself into was entirely up to him. Once the exchange was made, I would wash my hands of the whole thing. Including Mickey.

Of course, this was *before* the final piece of the puzzle had fallen into place, and the *real* star player stepped from the shadows and into the spotlight.

chapter ten

his final bow/beneath the mask/an equitable exchange

Dusk had already begun to fall by the time I'd reached the entrance of the long private road that led to The Black Otter. As I sped along the tree-lined drive, the last streaks of daylight that managed to cut through the thick canopy of crisscrossing overhead branches faded into hazy wisps, and the golden-purple sky finally gave way to blue darkness as the mansion came into view.

I pulled to a stop at the west curve of the circular drive, several yards past the main entrance, so that my car was pointed back toward the way I'd just come. I killed the engine and got out. I was debating whether or not to leave the door open—in case the need should arise for a hasty retreat—when the valet from my first visit came down the front steps and greeted me with a friendly smile.

"Good evening, Mr. Parker. We've been expecting—"

"Tell Mr. Grayson that I'm here."

The boy halted with a look of confusion, and I immediately corrected myself.

"Tell Mr. *Valley* that I'm here."

"He's waiting for you in the lounge, sir. If you will follow me—"

I shook my head. "No. You tell Mr. Valley that I'm waiting for him out here."

The confused expression returned briefly, and with it, a scarcely perceptible dark twinkle in the boy's eyes. Then the polite smile returned, and with a courteous nod the boy said, "As you wish, sir."

Once the valet was gone, I swept the grounds with a cautious eye, looking for anyone who might be lying in wait. But all was still and silent across the sprawling moonlit lawn. If guards had been stationed behind any of the towering topiary figures, they did well at keeping out of sight. And unless they were armed, I would have no problem getting back into my car and driving off before they could bridge the distance between the lawn and the circular drive.

I was still scanning the grounds when Matt Grayson came down the front steps. He was accompanied by an entourage of fit young men, a few of which I recognized from my previous visits, including the doorman with the broad shoulders and black pearl eyes. They were all dressed in standard Black Otter employee attire—white shirts, black trousers, smartly knotted ties, and tailored vests that accentuated their hard physiques. Only the doorman and Matt Grayson were dressed in jackets—the former in his standard black tuxedo with the white gold Omega pin on the lapel, the latter in an expensive-looking business suit with a blue silk tie a few shades darker than his eyes. Matt Grayson stopped before he reached me, leaving a comfortable distance between us. His entourage stopped a few paces behind him and fanned out, with neutral expressions on their well-scrubbed faces, like soldiers on the front line, awaiting their commander's signal.

"You made good time, Jack," he said as if this were a cordial meeting. "My apologies for the length of your stay at the police station. I hope it wasn't too uncomfortable."

I worked hard to steel my nerves as my eyes darted over the faces of the entourage. They stood like a row of statues, but I couldn't suppress the feeling that at any moment they might pounce.

Matt Grayson said calmly, "You needn't worry about Mr. Guerin. I can assure you that he won't be troubling you any further."

It wasn't me I was worried about when it came to Doug Guerin. But I didn't say anything. There was no way of telling for sure just how much Matt Grayson knew about the fight at the school. He might have assumed that I'd simply lost it under the pressure and taken out my buried aggression on a random parent who'd picked the wrong day to lodge a complaint at the school.

As I forced the rising fear back down, I tried to convince myself that Matt Grayson knew nothing about the situation between Shane and his father—and further, that he didn't know I'd thrown away my entire teaching career in defense of Shane Guerin.

There won't be any grace period or warning, Jack. They'll simply remove Mickey from the equation, and then find someone else that you care about.

Looking into Matt Grayson's eyes now, I had no trouble believing that he meant what he'd said to me the night before. If they discovered that Shane was someone who mattered to me, they would have no compunction about using him as leverage.

Matt Grayson allowed the silence to hover for a moment, then said, "I take it you've brought the package with you?"

I glanced over the line of young men again and said, "It's safe. Where's Mickey?"

Matt Grayson smiled politely. "He's in the lounge. I thought we would conduct this transaction like gentlemen. If you'd care to come inside . . . "

There was no guile in his pale blue eyes, but still I had no intention of going back inside The Black Otter.

I shook my head. "No. You bring him out here. Once I see that he's safe, I'll give you what you want."

He could have easily instructed his men to move in on me and take what he wanted by force, but he didn't. Instead, he tipped a nod to the doorman who headed back inside with two of the young men. I remained on guard while Matt Grayson continued to gaze at me with his calm blue eyes, as if studying an opponent of equal skill and cunning. I was starting to feel anxious when he spoke in a conversational tone.

"That was quite a number you did on Mr. Guerin at the school. I wouldn't have guessed you had it in you." A small smile curled at one corner of his mouth. "He's a pretty big guy. Worked black ops in the middle east—on the Q.T., of course, but still. Not the sort of man most would feel comfortable standing toe to toe with." He paused and chewed thoughtfully at his lip. "A man like that doesn't go down easy—unless he has a reason to." He paused again and shook his head. "He must have really set you off, eh?"

I remained silent. Matt Grayson released a soft sigh.

"No matter. Like I said, you won't have to worry about watching your back. Mr. Guerin and I came to an understanding this afternoon, and he has no intention of pursuing the matter, legally or otherwise."

He held his gaze on me for a moment longer, as if searching for a chink in the armor. A bead of cold sweat trickled down my back, but I did not avert my gaze from his.

The tension broke when the doorman and his boys came down the front steps of The Black Otter and headed across the drive toward us. There was a fourth person with them, tucked between the two younger men, but through the darkness and distance, I couldn't make out his face. Not until they'd reached the area on the driveway where moonlight spilled down on Matt Grayson and the rest of his entourage. Only then was I able to make positive ID.

It was Mickey. And he appeared to be unharmed. Shaken and scared, but unharmed.

My heart slammed in thunderous cymbal crashes when he called out to me. My first instinct was to rush forward to protect him, but somehow I held it together and kept my focus. The two young men on either side of Mickey held his arms so that he couldn't break free and run to me. When Mickey began to struggle fiercely, they drove him to his knees and twisted his arms behind his back, and again I had to force myself not to spring forward. Instead, I shot a hard glance at Matt Grayson, who immediately called out, "That's enough."

The struggling stopped, but the two guys holding Mickey didn't ease up until Matt Grayson gave them the cool edge of his gaze.

Then Mickey was looking up at me with trembling lips and tear-filled eyes. "I'm so sorry, Mr. M. I'm so so sorry. I never meant for you to get mixed up in this, you've got to believe me—"

One of the guys holding Mickey grabbed a handful of his hair and forced his head back. Mickey winced and stopped speaking at once.

Matt Grayson looked at me with cool purpose in his gaze. "As you can see, Jack, he's all in one piece and ready to go home with you. All we need to finalize this exchange is the contents of the safety deposit box."

My eyes shifted from Matt Grayson to Mickey and back again. There was no guarantee that either Mickey or I would be allowed to leave this place once I gave these men what they wanted. But there was no alternative, either.

I looked back at Mickey one last time before I turned to open the car door and reached into the back seat. For a second I imagined that the doorman and his minions would pounce the moment I came out with the gym bag, but when I turned around with the bag in hand, none of them had moved an inch. They stood as before, patiently waiting for the prize.

I looked into Matt Grayson's eyes, searching for a sign of the double-cross, but there was nothing remotely readable. Just that cool sea of impenetrable blue.

I pitched the bag forward. It landed on the pavement, roughly halfway between us, and the doorman came forward to collect it. He took it back to the line of young men and cradled it in his outstretched forearms. Matt Grayson unzipped the bag and rooted through its contents, feeling around all four sides with his fingers. When he came up empty-handed, he unzipped the pouches on both ends and searched them as well. He was in the process of checking the bag's single side pouch when I said, "You don't have to worry, it's all there."

He continued searching as if he hadn't heard me, and when he was finished, he closed all the zippers and tossed the bag back to me. It landed inches from my feet.

"We're not interested in the money, Jack. The money was Gordon's. And considering that he put your name on the safety deposit box, I'd say it's a pretty safe bet he meant for you to have it." He offered a small sly smile. "Of course, you could ship it to old Arthur C., the same as you did with those paintings—a noble but misguided act of honor—but then I'd just have to send somebody to collect it and return it to its rightful owner." He gestured with both hands to me, and then sighed. "And I'm fairly certain that old Arthur C. wouldn't be too happy about having to part with such a hefty sum of cash, so I'd likely have to do some serious convincing, which *could* get a little messy. So, it's probably best not to involve old Arthur C., who already has more money than anyone of his advanced age could ever hope to spend."

I remained silent, expecting the hammer to fall at any moment. Matt Grayson smiled like a teacher determined to help a favored student understand a difficult equation.

"Money isn't power, Jack. I've had all the money I could ever want or need since the day I was born, and, as you can see, it can buy a lot." He cast a leading glance at the towering mansion. Then his gaze returned to me. "But power—*real* power—isn't something you can buy. If you want it, you have to take it. By force, if necessary."

He paused again, and this time I could feel the wind as the hammer came down.

"Real power is that little memory stick you found in Gordon's safety deposit box this afternoon, along with all that free cash I'm going to let you walk away with once you hand the stick over. Or we can play it another way . . . "

He snapped his fingers, and immediately the doorman reached inside his jacket and pulled out a gun. In a smooth movement that only felt like slow motion, he pressed the muzzle against Mickey's head and cocked the hammer.

Matt Grayson smiled politely and said, "Please tell me you brought the stick with you, Jack."

The doorman's black eyes shined with purpose as his forefinger grazed the gun's trigger. I had no doubt that he was the sort of man who would follow orders without question. The only thing I wasn't entirely sure of was just *whose* orders he was following. I had an idea—one that I could scarcely credit, despite all that I'd discovered over the past several hours—and it was confirmed when Mickey suddenly spoke up.

"Don't do it, Mr. M—"

The doorman pressed the muzzle of the gun deeper into Mickey's temple, and Mickey gritted his teeth bravely—in perfect replication of a performance he'd given in my drama class back in his senior year. The scene had been from a play entitled *Sleuth*. Mickey had played the part of the handsome young man who is invited to a country estate by his lover's possessive husband. In the climactic moment, the kid who played the jealous husband pressed the muzzle of a gun to

Mickey's head and cocked the hammer, forcing Mickey to his knees, while Mickey bravely gritted his teeth. The scene did not end well for Mickey's character, but here on the circular drive of The Black Otter, my gut instinct told me that no gunshot would be ringing out.

You don't know him, Mr. McGregor, Marilyn Plath called out to me from the steps of the gymnasium on that long past awards night eve.

The boy is an apple-polisher, Jack, Gordon Powell chimed in from the smoky mist of the teacher's lounge.

It was a terrible risk, but I had to take it. I had to know the truth, once and for all.

I took a measured breath and said, "I'll give you the memory stick. But I want you to do something for me first. And it's nonnegotiable."

Matt Grayson chuckled. "Jack, I'll do anything for you. Name it."

But I wasn't speaking to Matt Grayson.

I was speaking to Mickey.

I was looking into his eyes, seeing past the well-constructed façade, past the intricate layers of the performance. Seeing the *real* Mickey Greenleaf, a kid who'd been raised in what appeared to be a positive environment with loving parents and yet somehow had turned into this cunning young man before me. Even down on his knees with a gun to his head, Mickey was in control. Just as he had been all those nights he'd sat on the couch in my apartment with tears in his eyes as he begged me to let him stay, if only for the night. And just as it had been back then, his performance on the drive outside The Black Otter on this warm spring night was undeniably impressive; his skills at the art of manipulation flawless.

The only thing that had changed was me.

I was no longer his captive audience. In the years that had gone between those days when I was green and

Mickey was golden, a significant measure of the magic had slipped away. The curtain had risen on the opposite side of the stage, where all those meticulously crafted fronts that looked so real from the perspective of the audience were revealed to be nothing more than painted canvas flats. Even the personal effects of the players were nothing more than props waiting to be returned to the storage cupboard once the show was over.

Thanks for believing in me . . .

I'm going to make you so proud . . .

Wait and see, things will be different when I come back . . .

Just pretend like it's all a dream, Mr. M. . . .

I held my gaze on Mickey, unwavering, unyielding, and found a strength within that until that moment I hadn't known I possessed. "I want you to show me. I want to see the real you. And if I don't, you can rest assured you will never get your hands on that memory stick." I took a deliberate pause before driving home the final nail: "Look me in the eye, Michael, and tell me that I'm lying."

The final leg of disillusionment came not in a dramatic outpouring of fiery emotion, complemented by a swelling of equally dramatic music, but rather like a velvet blade slid between the rib cage, gently piercing the heart, while a trusted face broke into a sweetly sad smile and those once adored lips parted to whisper: *It would have all been so perfect if you had just stayed in the dark and not gone rooting around my secret cupboard.*

Mickey gave a scarcely perceptible nod, and the two young men released him at once. As he got to his feet, he held out a hand. The doorman relinquished the gun to him and stepped back into line with the others. Then Mickey turned his head sideways until the bones in his neck emitted a satisfying series of pops. He did the same in the opposite direction, eliciting an even louder series of pops, as he shifted the gun from his left hand to his right and pointed it directly at me. It was a mimicry of a scene from one of his favorite movies, where the killer, having just revealed himself to his unsuspecting prey, takes the gun from her and tilts his head to pop the bones in his neck. I would have written it off as yet another performance in a long line of performances, but I was beginning to understand that this *particular* performance was as dangerously close to the real Mickey Greenleaf as I was ever going to get.

I was still waiting for him to speak when he did something unexpected. He pulled the trigger.

It happened so fast that I didn't even have time to flinch before the hammer came down with an anticlimactic click against the empty chamber.

Mickey handed the gun back to the doorman and kept his gaze on me as he addressed Matt Grayson. "I told you he'd come for me. He's been trying to save me ever since the day he met me in his fifth period drama class. He has a soft spot for abused strays, don't you, Mr. M." His eyes acquired a nostalgic glint. "I had him wrapped around my little finger back in the day. Anything I wanted, Mr. M. would move mountains to get it for me. Except for one thing . . . "

A shadow of melancholy flickered across his countenance, like an errant cloud passing over the moon. And then it was gone, replaced by a shrewd grin and a sly twinkle.

"Mr. M. was a true blue boy scout with unimpeachable integrity—and trust me, I tried to impeach it more than enough times to know. He took the bait, but I could never reel him in. I got close a time or two—that night I slipped into his bed, he wanted me so bad, he could taste it. He was like a schoolboy, trembling, ready to burst. But he couldn't pull the trigger. He's just not wired that way. You could lead him down a thousand easy paths to comfort and pleasure, and he'll veer off onto the one that's thick with thorns every time. It's in his blood. He'd sooner die of a thousand cuts than take a single decisive blow to his precious integrity."

I swallowed hard and resisted the urge to respond.

Mickey never liked sharing the spotlight anyway. He smiled at me, almost warmly, then his expression became serious.

"I need you to do something for me now, Mr. M. Something that'll be right up your alley because it's a rescue mission. I need you to ride in on your white horse and save the day. Only this time I'm going to *reward* you for your bravery. I'm going to give you something you're not even fully aware you want. How does that sound?"

I remained silent, but by the depth of his smile, I could tell that he'd read the minute shift in my eyes. Something dark flitted across his own eyes, but his expression remained pleasant.

"I know you went to see my folks today. And I know what you and my mom talked about in my room." He paused to study my reaction before going on. "She was very surprised and happy when I called her this evening. Of course, I had a lot of explaining to do because I haven't been in touch for a while. But you know me, I'm a resourceful kind of guy, and pretty soon she was telling me all about your little visit . . . and your interest in my freshman buddy from school." He dropped a sly wink. "You're quite the junior detective, Mr. M., putting together all those pieces of the puzzle on your own like that. I'm very proud of you. Gold stars straight down the board. But then you did have a *little* help from me—or at least from my past mistakes. I should have known that sooner or later Shane would find his way into your heart. That kid had the biggest crush on you back in his freshman year—not that you would have noticed. Back then he was just a scrawny little shit, but, man, did he fill out over the past five years!" He dropped another wink, with a lascivious grin. "Gotta be hard resisting *that* sort of temptation . . . even for a super straight-arrow boy scout like you, eh, Mr. M.?"

I could feel the muscles in my jaw tensing, but I didn't take the bait. Mickey's grin faded into a wistful smile.

"I suppose that's why he trusted me. Because he knew

how tight you and I were. I had to practically drag the shit about his dad out of him, but he was very forthcoming about his feelings for you. Oh, he didn't tell me all about it straight off—you know how he is. But with a little detective work of my own, I eventually got inside his head and discovered all his little secret desires. He had a real Batman and Robin thing for you. It was actually kind of sweet. We used to role-play when he'd spend the night at my house. I'd play you, and come to his rescue. And then we'd snuggle under the covers in our underwear. He'd call me Jack and lay his head on my chest and tell me that he knew I'd come and save him, and I'd hold him in my arms until he fell asleep."

I felt a sudden wave of anger mixed with revulsion, and my body tensed. Mickey held up his open palms as if to say no harm, no foul. But the grin that accompanied the gesture appeared to indicate otherwise.

"Take it easy, Mr. M., I didn't pop his cherry. Contrary to what his old man would have thought, it was all very innocent." His eyes shined dimly with nostalgia. "And once I'd earned his trust, it was pretty easy to draw out his inner Rufus. And as we both know, Rufus has no problem speaking his mind."

Mickey chuckled at the reaction he'd elicited from me with this unexpected nugget, and my cheeks burned.

"Relax, Mr. M.," he said with a wink. "I won't tell if you won't tell. It was just another little exercise in role-playing. A confidence booster. We made a deal that whenever he was away from school, he'd forget his crappy home life and be like any other kid. So when we'd go out to the mall or the movies or the skate park, he'd forget Shane and become Rufus, because Rufus was a cool and easy going guy, with zero strife and zero worries, whose main objective was to just be a kid and have a good time. And no, I didn't brainwash him or anything. He made Rufus up all on his own. I just told him that his character had to come from a genuine place inside and that he couldn't fake it—just like you taught us in drama class, Mr. M., remember? You said, 'Acting is a noble art—just don't ever let your audience catch you doing it.' Remember?"

I remembered. It had been the "money line" of my opening lecture to all of my drama classes over the past five years. But I certainly hadn't meant for Mickey, or any other student, to apply it in real life.

As if reading my thoughts, Mickey said, "I'm not blaming you, Mr. M.—I'm *thanking* you. I learned more from you than all of my other teachers put together—with the obvious exception of old Gordon Powell, of course."

My eyes narrowed, and Mickey laughed.

"Let's not get carried away, Mr. M. I know old Gordon was your father figure—and judging by the stacks he left for you in his bank box, he clearly had a soft spot for you—but don't have any illusions that Gordon was in control here. He didn't bring *me* into the fold. *I'm* the one who brought *him* into it. Not that he had anything to complain about. He was more than happy to take the money."

"The money from the art scam," I said, sensing that we were finally getting down to the crux.

This time it was Mickey who looked confused. But only for a moment.

"The art scam, eh?"

He cracked a half-smile, then shot a glance at Matt Grayson whose expression was unreadable. When Mickey turned back to me, he was no longer smiling.

"I need to ask you a question, and I'll know if you're lying—and trust me, Mr. M., you don't want to do that." He paused to let the message sink in, then said, "Did you happen to plug that little memory stick into a computer and have a quick peek before you came here?"

Matt Grayson interjected calmly, "The files are all encrypted."

Mickey ignored him and repeated the question. "Did you attempt to see the contents of the flash drive, Mr. M.?"

I met his gaze and said, "No, I did not."

It wasn't a lie, but it wasn't the whole truth either. Given the argument I'd overheard between Mr. Dorian Grey and Matt Grayson the night before, I had a fairly good idea of what the contents of the flash drive might be. At the back of my mind I could hear Mr. Gray shouting: *You calm down, this is my fucking political life we're talking about here—and the lives of a lot of other decent people as well.* But I didn't let on that I had any memory of what had been going on around me while I was drugged and strapped down to the table in the white room.

Mickey wasn't finished. "Did you make a copy of the files on the flash drive?"

Without taking my eyes from his, I shook my head. His gaze intensified for a moment, then his features relaxed and he nodded. He shot one more look at Matt Grayson before turning his attention back to me.

"I'm going to tell you what I need you to do, Mr. M., and then I'm going to tell you what I'm going to give you in return—and despite any notion you may have to the contrary, these terms are nonnegotiable." He paused briefly. "If you fail to accept this offer, I am going to call the men who are watching Shane Guerin at this very moment, and they are going to move in on him. They won't harm him, but they will bring him here, where he will be stripped naked and strapped down to the bench in the Sigma room for a demonstration of what happens when I don't get what I want. And you, Mr. M., will have a front-row seat in the viewing room . . . and this time, it won't be a performance. It will be the real thing—and by comparison, it will make what Shane's father has done to him look like a lovely dream." He paused again, then added. "Now look me in the eye, Jack, and tell me that *I'm* lying."

I could feel the muscles in my jaw tensing as Mickey's eyes shimmered coolly in the streaks of moonlight that cut through the overhead branches of a towering oak just off the drive. And for a short-lived half-second, it was as if Mickey and I were the only two people on the endless grounds of The Black Otter—as if Matt Grayson and his entourage of pretty thugs had simply ceased to exist, or stepped off into the shadowy recesses, like ghosts.

In that split-second that seemed to last for an eternity, I could see the two of us, Mickey and I, like players on a stage—or combatants in an arena—facing off. I could see the stunned look of disbelief in his eyes as the first blow landed, knocking him to the pavement. I could see the fear in those eyes as I pounced and began raining blows upon him. I could hear him gasping for breath as my fingers tightened around his throat. I could hear the sickening cracking sound as I drove his head into the pavement repeatedly until his arms stopped flailing and his body went limp. And as the final spasms slowly sputtered out and I removed my hands from his purple throat, a supreme sense of relief flooded my senses, because in that moment, in that finite fraction in time, I could see that the pitiful mess gazing up at me through those dying eyes was the real Mickey Greenleaf. And like any other magnificent creature of mythical stature, in the final throes, he was no longer larger than life.

The moment passed like a facile whisper on a gentle breeze, and with it came the understanding that I would offer no further resistance. I'd gotten what I'd come here for. Mickey had finally removed his mask. And though some small nostalgic part of me would have liked to go on believing in the fantasy that Mickey had spun out of whole cloth back in that blissfully ignorant time when I still believed I could actually make a difference as a teacher, I was relieved to see the curtain come down on the final act at last. I was ready to leave the theater and let the entire experience fade into memory where it belonged.

With that thought, I did not wait for further instruction from my former pupil. I reached into my pocket and took out the memory stick. I held it up, and when Mickey nodded,

Matt Grayson stepped forward to retrieve it. But just as he reached out, I closed my fingers around the memory stick and looked into Mickey's eyes. I suppose I was going to say something like, "I have your word, right?" or "Promise me that it ends here" or "Swear to me that you'll leave Shane Guerin out of this." But I didn't say any of those things, because it would have been pointless to attempt to secure a guarantee from one who possessed no moral code.

The ghost of a smile curled at one corner of Mickey's mouth, as if he'd read my thoughts, and, further, that he concurred with my assessment. In that defining moment, the long-standing illusion that there had ever been anything genuine between us was dispelled.

I handed the memory stick over to Matt Grayson. He nodded in return, then snapped his fingers.

Immediately the doorman broke from the ranks and came forward at such a brisk pace I didn't even have enough time to think any of the last thoughts that supposedly run through the frantic minds of the doomed at the moment of truth, things like *This is it,* or *It ends right here,* or *I know too much and now they have to get rid of me*, or even that old standard *Oh shit!*

My body tensed, ready for a losing battle, but the doorman simply picked up the gym bag at my feet, took it to my car, and placed it on the floor behind the driver's seat. Then he returned to the line of young men.

I stood motionless, unsure of what to do.

Then Mickey spoke again. "That's it, Mr. M. You can go now."

When I still didn't move, Mickey released a soundless laugh and shook his head, as if he was now the teacher and I his reluctant pupil.

"Contrary to what you think of me, Mr. M., I'm not a complete monster. I do have a *modicum* of integrity. And I honor my word. You held up your end of the bargain, and now I'm going to hold up mine. You'll find what I promised you in the theater at the school—call it my parting gift to you." He allowed a small smile, one that seemed a bit sad and tinged with regret. "But I wouldn't put off retrieving it till morning. If you want it, you'd better go get it tonight. Trust me, Mr. M., this is not something you want falling into the wrong hands. You're in enough trouble with the school board as it is. No need to invite any further complication into the mix." He shrugged. "But that's entirely up to you. In any case, the money in that bag can give you a fresh start anyplace you choose . . . anyplace but here." The smile remained, but it no longer looked sad or regretful. "Our business here is done, Mr. M. This is the last time I expect to see you. Do I make myself clear?"

I didn't respond, but he could see in my eyes that all was perfectly clear and that I had no intention of testing him.

"Then I wish you the best," he said. And with that, he turned and walked back toward the stone steps leading up to the wide veranda. From there, he disappeared through the open double doors, like a performer exiting the stage for the last time.

As I drove away from The Black Otter, I imagined Mickey watching from the window of the highest room, like the prince in the tower from some old faerie tale whose pages I'd last turned in simpler days. It was just a flight of fancy, one that came in a brief flicker and was gone even before I'd turned onto the main road that led back to the highway.

After that night, I never saw Mickey Greenleaf again.

epilogue

let the right one in

It was late when I finally pulled into the reserved slot in front of my apartment building. I'd resolved to head straight home from The Black Otter and ignore the temptation of Mickey's "parting gift." But the more I tried to push it out of my thoughts, the more difficult it was to resist.

You'll find what I promised you in the theatre at the school. I wouldn't put off retrieving it till morning. If you want it, you'd better go get it tonight.

I might have been able to let it go, if not for the appended caveat . . .

Trust me, Mr. M., this is not something you want falling into the wrong hands. You're in enough trouble with the school board as it is. No need to invite any further complication into the mix.

As it turned out, no further complication was required to cement the school board's decision. There was a brief glimmer of hope when both Principal Suarez and Marthe Derderian stepped up to testify on my behalf, but after the security footage was leaked on the web, my employment at West High was terminated by a unanimous vote. Still, had the gift Mickey left for me in the theater that night happened to fall into the wrong hands, it would have certainly opened a whole other can of worms. And not just for me, but for Shane Guerin as well. The local press had already had a field day with the story of the teacher who'd assaulted the abusive parent of one of his students, but they were still hungry for more. And Mickey's little parting gift would have given them plenty to feed on.

The school was deserted when I pulled up to the loading dock. The side door was locked, but I had a key and let myself in. The left wing was cloaked in shadow, but a thin line of light shone from under the black curtains which separated the main stage from the backstage area. When I stepped through the divide in the curtain, I saw what Mickey had left for me. In his typical dramatic fashion, he'd placed it on a stool beneath a cool blue spotlight, center stage.

Though the house was dark and silent, I couldn't help feeling a little apprehensive as I crossed the stage and stepped into the circle of light, like an actor who'd suddenly forgotten all of his lines. But this was a silent show for an empty theatre, where my visceral response was all that was required. As I gazed down at the prize on the stool, I was struck by the ease with which Mickey could still manipulate my emotions, and more than a bit unnerved by the canny accuracy of his strike.

I closed my eyes and pushed back against the encroaching tide within, and when it receded, I looked down at the stool, upon which three items were neatly laid. At the bottom of the stack was what, to the casual eye, would have appeared to be an old notebook. But it wasn't. It was a sketchbook, and I didn't have to look at the name on the inside flap to know who it had once belonged to. The next item was the remote control for the theatre's sound system, with a little sticky note attached that read PRESS PLAY. The third item was a shiny red apple, centered perfectly atop the sketchbook, like the deleterious offering in the penultimate act of a faerie tale.

There was a part of me that wanted to turn and walk away, deny Mickey his final moment in the spotlight, and never look back. But as it always had been with Mickey, my resolve was defeated by my curiosity.

I pressed the PLAY button on the remote control, and within seconds music began to spill from the speakers, filling the auditorium. It was a song by Collective Soul—one that was forever etched into my memory, as it was the same song that Mickey had used for his final in my drama class. The assignment was for each student to create a short solo video of his or her vision of life after high school. Most of the class did mock interviews, like video selfies, in which they spoke of the ups and downs of life in the grown-up world. Mickey, however, took a different approach and made an artistic black and white video of himself walking through his past childhood haunts in a somber sort of limbo, uncertain, apprehensive about crossing over the invisible line between boyhood and manhood.

Unlike the other students, Mickey did not speak a word in his video. The entire soundtrack was dubbed over with the Collective Soul song. A couple of his peers dared to call him out for turning the assignment into nothing more than a "glorified music video," but most agreed that Mickey's video was the best in the class. One of his defenders praised him for not going with the more obvious choices of Collective Soul's two biggest hits, *Run* and *The World I Know*. I couldn't have agreed more with this assessment.

The song Mickey had chosen for the soundtrack of his video was *Crown*, a poignant tune whose melancholy lyrics spoke to a truth that was perhaps beyond the scope of the average teenage experience, and yet it underscored the theme of Mickey's video perfectly with its existential ruminations of one facing one's own impending mortality. Like a fading monarch with no heir apparent, Mickey wandered aimlessly through the bleak landscape of his colourless kingdom on screen, accompanied only by those haunting lyrics . . .

I hope I'm not lost,
but I think that hope is now distancing,
and the words that secure a cause
are now faint whisperings . . .

As those lyrics invaded my senses, I began to flip through the pages of the sketchbook. Most of the drawings had been rendered in greyscale with charcoal sticks (or Conté crayons, as Gordon would have more accurately referred to them), though a smattering featured splashes of colour here and there. All were stunningly lifelike and realized by a skilled hand.

I pictured that skilled hand moving deftly over this sketchbook while the eyes beneath the cascade of long bangs focused effortlessly on each stroke. It was a scene I'd witnessed on countless occasions back in my first year teaching at West High: a fourteen-year-old freshman, tall for his age, unassumingly handsome, sitting in his seat of the back of my classroom, quietly drawing in his sketchbook while most of his classmates were still working on the assignment he'd finished in half the time.

A sudden wave of tendrils raced my spine as the simple truth settled in. The drawings that the shy boy had been working on at the back of my classroom five years ago were the very same I was looking at now.

The signature at the bottom of each page was small and tight, as if the artist had been too modest to take credit for his own work. But halfway through the sketchbook, the signature had changed. Though the handwriting was the same, the name was different. And more prominently displayed.

And with the new name came a bolder, more assertive artistic style. The greyscales were deeper, with layers of complexity and emotion that practically leapt from the page; the spot use of colour was at once more striking yet subtle.

And almost all of these drawings were of one subject.

Me.

Sitting at my desk, reading a book or grading papers while the class worked on the day's written assignment. Standing at the blackboard while giving a lecture. Leaning back against the front edge of my desk while thoughtfully listening to one of the students during a class discussion. A profile angle of me stooping down in the aisle to assist a student in the front row with a problem on her paper.

But none of these were the sort of drawings that would have invited "further complication into the mix," as Mickey had pointedly put it. They were all innocuous images that wouldn't have raised so much as a single brow, even amongst the more provincial members of the school board.

It was the drawings closer to the end of the sketchbook that would have thrown up red flags in droves—beginning with one of me at the faculty-student soccer match, in which my stomach and chest are exposed as I lift my T-shirt to wipe sweat from my face, and culminating with several images of Mickey and me in compromising positions, including one of the two of us holding hands, our lips touching, our eyes closed, both of us naked.

While the image of me on the soccer pitch was drawn from real life, the others were solely products of the imagination that had most likely found their way from Shane's skilled hand to his sketchbook by way of the gentle art of coercion that Mickey Greenleaf had honed to perfection.

Trust me, Mr. M., this is not something you want falling into the wrong hands.

The thought of placing my trust in Mickey Greenleaf brought a bitter lump to my throat, one that I swallowed back because—if only on this single issue—I could not deny that Mickey was correct. The last thing I wanted or needed was for this sketchbook to fall into the wrong hands. If nothing else, my experience with Mickey had taught me well how easily one's perception can eclipse the truth.

The last image in the sketchbook was both jarring and heartbreaking at once. It featured Shane under the covers in his bed. From every darkened corner of the room, hungry creatures were being held at bay by a force field, which appeared to be flowing from the outstretched hands of the figure who stood vigil at Shane's bedside. Though this protector looked more like a superhero in a comic book than a man from real life, the facial features were undeniably my own. With my hair hanging a bit longer than normal and my face painted chalk white, Shane had drawn me as a Crow-like defender, powerful enough to keep the demons from descending upon him while he slept. Powerful enough to also hold off the shadowy figure in the bedroom doorway—an ominous figure that, judging by his size and shape, could have only been Doug Guerin.

For a second I couldn't breathe; my eyes felt warm and wet. At the same time Shane had been filling this sketchbook with these images, Mickey had been filling me with lies that would live for nearly five years before reaching the light of day. And I had swallowed them all, never once stopping to question him. Never once stopping to open my eyes and really see the other boy, that fourteen-year-old kid at the back of my freshman English class confiding his secrets in his sketchbook. Looking to me as a protector, and getting no response.

Because you were too busy responding to the apple-polisher, Jack, Gordon Powell chimed in.

I shook my head, but not in dismissal of the accusation.

It would have been easy to lay the blame on Mickey, who'd known exactly what was going on in Shane's house, and not only turned a blind eye to it but used the information Shane had entrusted him with for his own personal gain. But Mickey had only been a kid himself back then. A full four years older than Shane, but still just a kid. I had been the responsible party and should have recognized what was going on. With both Mickey and Shane.

Had I followed my first instinct and confronted Mickey's father straightaway, I would have discovered the truth right then and there. And maybe, with a little help from his parents, who appeared to be kind and decent people, I might have been able to get Mickey to tell me where he'd come up with his outlandish tales of abuse. Of course, Mickey had begged me not to get involved, arguing that he would be leaving for college soon and would never again have to be subjected to his father's "abuse." And at the time, it made sense. He was eighteen and legal, and the choice had been his to make.

But for Shane things had been very different. His tales of abuse had not been borrowed and revamped for the sole purpose of gaining sympathy and trust. The abuse he'd suffered at the hands of his father had been real. Real enough to put him in traction for eight months and add another year to his sentence at home.

And all of it could have been avoided, had I only removed the blinders and done what any responsible adult would have done.

As I looked down at the sketchbook in my hands, I wondered how many times I'd seen it back when it was still a work in progress. How many times had Shane left it where I could have easily picked it up and perused its telling pages? Had I ever once pulled Shane aside when he'd shown up at school with a fresh bruise, or a black eye, or a cast on one of his limbs? Had I ever once considered tearing my focus away from Mickey long enough to see what was going on around me?

Just pretend like it's all a dream, Mr. M.

But it wasn't all a dream. I was wide awake and ready to face the music.

It wasn't Mickey who was to blame. It was me. In the end, it all came back to me, and there was no one else to blame.

The last few pages of the sketchbook were blank, and affixed to the center of the final page was another sticky note. It read:

The mind has a thousand eyes,
And the heart but one . . .

And below that:

You have a second chance to get things right—
Don't make the same mistake twice.
—MKG

I flipped back to the final drawing, the one in which Shane lay asleep under the covers while I stood guard at his bedside. As I looked down at this hopeful image, the final bars of the Collective Soul song faded, and in the silence that followed I could have almost sworn that I heard Mickey calling from that not-so-distant past we once shared, echoing the chorus in a mournful whisper one last time . . .

Who's gonna wear my crown . . . ?

The song was still running through my mind as I sat motionless behind the wheel of my car, gazing blankly at the darkened dashboard. On the floor behind my seat, there was a bag filled with cash, Gordon's legacy to me. Yet all I could think about was the dog-eared sketchbook on the seat beside me. It sat there like a silent indictment, daring me to deny the charges contained within.

As I looked up at the darkened window of my apartment, I understood that it would be impossible to head up the stairs and collapse onto my bed. Not after all that had happened today. I couldn't just turn a blind eye and get on with my life—whatever life I would have left after the school board was done with me. What I needed now wasn't sleep, and it certainly wasn't what inevitably would come with sleep. I'd been chasing a ghost in a dream since shortly after Gordon's death—the same ghost in the same dream that I'd been lost in ever since the first day I'd laid eyes on the unattainable Mickey Greenleaf. Unattainable because I had been his teacher at the time and truly believed that some lines could not be crossed.

But right now I wasn't anyone's teacher. I'd been suspended for the remainder of the school year, and more than likely I would not be returning for the fall semester. And that meant I was free to follow my own conscience.

I could still hear the promise Matt Grayson had made to me only hours before as we stood face to face on the circular drive out front of The Black Otter.

You needn't worry about Mr. Guerin. I can assure you that he won't be troubling you any further.

But it wasn't *my* safety that concerned me.

In a sudden rush, the voices of Doug Guerin and Mickey Greenleaf came like a verbal sparring match in my mind . . .

I know your weakness, Jack.

His eyes . . . like the eyes of those white wolves . . . I swear it, Mr. M.

A boy needs discipline, eh, Jack?

That kid had the biggest crush on you, Mr. M.

Once he comes home—and, trust me, he's got no other place to go—

I should have known that sooner or later Shane would find his way into your heart.

—I'm gonna make him pay.

You have a second chance to get things right.

And this time there won't be a visible mark on him—I'm very proficient at what I do, Jack.

Don't make the same mistake twice, Mr. M.

I wasn't sure if what I was about to do was yet another mistake, but I had to do something.

It was already after eleven, and the bistro where Shane worked closed at ten, so it was a good bet that he was either already home or on his way there. I hoped it was the latter, or that possibly Kaitlin, the girl he worked with, had talked him into meeting up with friends after they'd closed up shop, because if he was already home, it might be too late.

I pushed back on that final thought and told myself that Shane was all right, that his father was in no shape to do any harm to him anytime soon. After the beating he'd taken at the school, not to mention the visit from Matt Grayson and his crew, Doug Guerin would likely still be licking his wounds. But as with any injured animal, there was always the possibility that he might strike—particularly with a more vulnerable creature in his immediate proximity.

I was ready to fire up the engine and head straight out to Shane's house, but I stopped short when a sudden realization dawned. I was possibly about to come face to face with the man I'd attacked this afternoon, and depending on his response—fight or flight—there was a chance that the police could be called in again. Being picked up by the police twice on the same day would be bad enough. Having them discover the gym bag full of money—not to mention the sketchbook full of risqué drawings of me, done by a then-underage student—would be far worse.

I needed to get rid of both before I headed out to Shane's place.

I took the gym bag from the back seat, opened it, and tucked the sketchbook inside with the money. I got out of my car and headed to the entrance at a brisk pace. It would only take a moment to drop the bag inside my apartment, and then I would be on my way.

As I climbed the stairs, with the bag's strap over my shoulder, I attempted to calm my racing heart by telling myself that everything was going to be all right, that when Matt Grayson had told me I had nothing to worry about, it meant that Shane had nothing to worry about either. Because Shane would be under the same blanket of protection that had been provided for me, because Mickey knew that I cared about Shane and that any harm done to him would be the same—even greater—than harm done directly to me. I told myself that Mickey had made a deal with me: Shane's safety in exchange for the memory stick. I'd held up my end of the deal, and surely Mickey would hold up his.

Suddenly I could hear Mickey's voice inside my head—not the real Mickey, but a cunning spectre of him, whispering with a delicious chuckle: *I told you that* I *wouldn't harm him, Mr. M. I never said anything about his old man. You're Batman, it's your job to save Robin. Hurry, Mr. M. The clock is ticking.*

I halted abruptly at the top of the stairs, and my heart stopped for what seemed an infinite time. I stood there like a statue, unable or unwilling to comprehend what was waiting for me at the end of the hall.

It was the figure of a teenage boy slumped against the wall opposite my apartment door. Knees pulled up close to his chest, arms wrapped around his folded legs, face buried in the cleft of his knees. Posed like Rodin's Thinker. But not naked. He was dressed in the same T-shirt and jeans he'd been wearing when I last saw him, earlier today in my third period English class. Only now he was still and silent, as if at rest.

Somewhere at the back of my mind I could hear the distant echo of Mickey's promise: *I'm going to give you something you're not even fully aware you want, Mr. M.*

And then suddenly my legs were no longer frozen, and I was moving slowly toward the figure at the end of the hall.

My heart began to beat again, pumping blood in a near-dizzying thrust straight to my head, when I got close enough to see the gentle rising and falling of the back beneath the T-shirt. Though his face remained buried against his knees and his eyes shrouded by his bangs, he'd heard my approach and knew that he was no longer alone. His back rose with a deep breath that came out in a ragged sigh, and after a long moment, he finally spoke.

"My dad kicked me out," he said, softly. Then his voice became choked with emotion. "I didn't know where else to go. I'm sorry."

When I bent down and placed a hand on his shoulder, he began to tremble, but he didn't cry. It was only after I'd put an arm around him and felt him leaning into my embrace that the tears finally began to flow. I couldn't deny the feeling of *déjà vu* that crept at the periphery of my thoughts. But at the same time, I understood something was very different, that I was not reliving one of the myriad scenes that had played out in this same apartment building five years ago with Mickey.

It came to me in a sudden yet subtle realization, after the tears had subsided and Shane had accepted my hand and allowed me to help him to his feet. It came in a stark contrast: While Shane had kept his head down in a brave attempt to contain his emotion, even as that emotion threatened to consume him, Mickey had never failed to look me directly in the eye . . . as if to make certain that I wouldn't miss a single tear.

This poignant juxtaposition would have likely brought a twinkle of amusement to Gordon Powell's eyes. But for me, it brought something entirely different. For me, it brought long overdue closure to an extended chapter of my life that was best left in the past, and real hope for a future, whatever that future might hold.

As this final thought drifted from my mind—and the last tenuous tether between myself and Mickey Greenleaf was cut—I unlocked the door and let Shane in.

Made in the USA
Middletown, DE
20 July 2019